INTERNS & VOLUNTEERS: Peter Rednour, Annie Wyman, Elizabeth Baird, Nick Buttrick, Jennifer King, Ally-Jane Grossan, Jesse Nathan, Alyssa Varner, Gwendolyn Roberts, Flynn Berry, Kristopher Doyle, Claire Powell, Teresa Maria Cotsirilos, Sophie Klimt, Sharareh Lotfi, Susie Pitzen, Jay Whiteside, Autumn Bayes, Christopher Benz, Elissa Bassist, Darren Franich, Katie MacBride, Graham Weatherly, Ian MacLean, Christina Rush, Claire Donato, Rachel Lane, Amy Horton, Rachel Gibson, Emily Aldana, Max Besbris. ALSO HELPING: Alvaro Villanueva, Chris Ying, Michelle Quint, Greg Larson, Barb Bersche. COPY EDITORS: Caitlin Van Dusen, Oriana Leckert. EDITORS-AT-LARGE: Gabe Hudson, Lawrence Weschler, Sean Wilsey. WEBSITE: Ed Page and Chris Monks. OUTREACH: Angela Petrella and Adam Krefman. CIRCULATION: Heidi Meredith. MANAGING EDITOR: Jordan Bass. PUBLISHER: Eli Horowitz. EDITOR: Dave Eggers.

NEW STORIES FROM OUR SHORES

FROM OUR SHORES

—part two of—

MCSWEENEY'S 26

CONTENTS

("Pentimento" and "Porcus Omnivorus" appear in two parts—
the final section of each story can be found in this book. It's best to start at
the beginning, in this issue's book of New Stories from Overseas.)

WINTER HIKE, *by Fred Simper, Jr. (Aberdeen Proving Ground, Md.)*

ARKANSAS

This piece is taken from John Brandon's novel Arkansas, *our newest McSweeney's Rectangular and the deep-southern drug trade's ticket to literary immortality. The novel follows Kyle and Swin, two young men who have abandoned unsatisfying lives to work as couriers for a man named Frog. Robert Olmstead has called it "a proud debut, a coup de main, a true feat of strength, power, and skill. John Brandon's on fire," he says, "every sentence a kill shot." You can read more about Brandon on this book's back cover;* Arkansas *can be found (soon, if not already) wherever fine books are sold.*

When Kyle arrived at the lot, he saw a flatbed truck. He'd never operated anything bigger than a van, and had to hide his nervousness over this fact when a beige guy appeared and said his name was Swin. The guy tried to make small talk, but Kyle kept quiet until they were on the interstate. Something was up. The day before, Colin had told Kyle he'd have a partner for this run, something he'd never had before. Colin had told Kyle that a gun would be provided in the vehicle's center console, something which had never been provided before, and now

written by John Brandon

the vehicle turns out to be a flatbed truck. Kyle didn't like the idea of having guns around when a deal was being made. He didn't know if Swin knew about the gun and didn't want to check the console with him watching. Kyle took a good look at the guy. He was a weights freak, with little muscles popping up where they shouldn't, on the back of his neck or his fingers. His T-shirt was a size too small.

"What kind of name is Swin?"

"A girl's," Swin said.

The load was faucets, more than a hundred cases, stuffed with bags of powder and plugged. This was another thing: Kyle knew what he was hauling. The way Frog ran his operation, his drivers simply drove a car to one place, got in another car, drove somewhere else. Sometimes the drivers handled money, sometimes not. Sometimes when Kyle returned to Little Rock he stopped off at Gregor's and unloaded something, sometimes not. Kyle preferred to be kept in the dark, but Colin had made a point to tell him about the faucets. Of course, he'd left out the amount. He hadn't let Kyle know he'd be captaining a highway barge.

Besides the faucets, Swin had also thrown on some miniature orange cones because, he explained, the randomness might throw off a cop. Their destination was South Padre, Texas. At a red light, rain started. Kyle knew the boxes wouldn't stay dry with Swin's shoddy cover job, so they pulled into a shopping center that included a hardware depot. The truck took two spaces. While Swin went for a tarp, Kyle bought rope and hurried back to the truck. He flipped open the console and there was the gun, reclined on sugar packets and ink pens and a tire gauge. Swin returned and they did their best with a roll of blue plastic that was meant to protect a small fishing boat. They got moving again and hit I-30. Swin took off his shirt and draped it on the seat to dry. A plus sign was tattooed on his right bicep, a minus sign on his left. Kyle asked if the left arm was weaker.

"It takes both for a charge. Step to me, you catch the voltage."

Kyle knew he could beat Swin up. "I've never wanted a tattoo," he said. "I've never

seen one that didn't look stupid."

"You're not a sexy dude. If you're already sexy, a tattoo can enhance it."

"Don't tell me you're one of those witty people."

"I've been told that I am."

"You remind me of a game-show host."

"That's another way to say I'm brimming with charisma."

"No," Kyle said. "It's not."

"If you want to be the strong, silent type, you need to keep yourself from commenting on things."

Kyle tipped his chin back until his neck cracked. "It won't be right away, but at some point I'm going to knock you on your ass."

"You say that now, but soon we'll be

friends. Everyone who meets me wants to be my friend."

Noonish they got a booth in a Southwestern restaurant with World Book place mats. Kyle's described belomancy, a process by which local Indians read the future by shooting arrows. Swin's was about Ford v. Wainwright, the ruling that made it unlawful to execute a crazy man. Kyle ordered a #7 combo. Swin was picky—didn't eat sour cream and didn't eat guacamole unless it was fresh. He and the waitress discussed what "fresh" meant. A woman with a baby sat down in a nearby booth and began nursing.

"That's good to see," Swin said.

"You're sad."

"A lot of women don't breast-feed anymore, which is a shame. Breast-fed kids get fewer syndromes. I was a formula baby. You, I'm guessing, had a mouthful of the real deal."

"No idea," Kyle said.

"Yup, I think you did."

"I lied about my mother once to get out of trouble with a girl. What do you think of that?"

"How much trouble?"

"Does it matter?"

"Is your mother in trouble now?"

"She's dead."

"Because you lied about her?"

"No. She's been dead."

Swin looked toward the ceiling, thinking. "A conversation this vague, really no point in having it."

"She was a great lady," said Kyle. "*Great* lady." He ate a chip.

"When people act sappy after someone's dead, that means they feel guilty."

"What do I feel guilty about?"

"How would I know?"

"I was always good to her."

"Not guilty about how they treated the person; guilty to have life and not know what to do with it."

When Kyle envisioned his mother, she was in a white bed, bandages on her left elbow and wrist where the shock had burnt off the skin, fingertips black, head shaved. Her face looked as though she'd been informed of a rude change of plans. Kyle would return from a walk to find her arms in a different position, and always it was just that a nurse had shifted her. Each Wednesday, he'd put her favorite program on, a game show about finding fake bombs. He began to settle into a routine, to get used to having his mother that way. It wasn't a bad way to be. She'd made an escape. For a time, Kyle hadn't wanted her to die or wake up, but to remain in peace, away from her life.

Swin opened a travel-size lotion and rubbed some on his elbows. "If one of my sisters died, I wouldn't care."

"What a stupid thing to say."

"I just don't care for women."

Kyle stared.

"I like them for *that*," said Swin.

"How about we both shut up."

They munched on chips for a time and slurped their drinks, the restaurant filling with nurses. Swin pointed without raising his hand off the table. "Caregivers."

They weren't far past Dallas before the tarp came loose again. They pulled into a truck stop and bought duct tape. The boxes were fraying. They did what they could with the tarp and got back on the highway, Kyle staying in the right lane and doing five over.

When Swin woke up, the sun was setting and the rain had stopped. He pulled the map out and did some measuring with his fingers. "If we go eighty-three the rest of the way, we won't be late."

"Getting pulled over with drugs makes you *really* late."

Swin looked over more maps from the glove box. There was one for each state, plastic booklets. "Here I go again," he said. "I'm learning again. You don't get this smart by accident."

The sky became a weak yellow, then abruptly it was night. They got off the interstate at a cluster of fast-food restaurants that all shared one lot, and parked in the far corner. They chose an all-you-can-eat restaurant where waitresses circled with bowls of pasta and salad and breadsticks. Kyle ate himself stunned. He planned to sleep away a good chunk of the remaining drive. The check came, with two peppermints, and he took care of it. Kyle and

Swin were chewing the mints when they walked outside and saw a tall bald man snooping around the truck. He leaned over and peeked under the tarp. The man wasn't dressed as a cop, but he had a badge patched on his sleeve. Kyle told Swin to do the talking. When they got close, the guy stood up past straight, hand to his chin. Swin shook his hand and introduced himself as Mike. Kyle said, "Hey, now," then climbed in the cab.

"First-aid kit's in the seat console," Swin yelled.

He knew about the gun. Kyle kept still and listened. The guy's name was Pat Bright. He was some kind of ranger.

"Headed far?"

"Corpus Christi," Swin told him.

"I noticed your rig needs some help."

"Not sure I agree with that a hundred percent. Though all things give out eventually, don't they? If you're patient." Swin's voice was even.

Kyle opened the console and lifted out the loaded nine-millimeter with two fingers. "What's better for a headache?" he called. "Tylenol or—" he tucked the gun under his leg, "Aleve?"

"Got to get more rope," Pat Bright was telling Swin. "Go corner to corner."

"We were in a hurry this morning. Still are."

"What's the haul?"

"Faucets. Some computer tycoon's place. Used to be oil, now it's computers."

"There's no faucets in Corpus Christi?"

"He's got to have that adobe-marble core."

Kyle pushed the mirror out and saw Bright beaming with tolerance.

"Let me take a look how you've got them stacked," Bright said.

"How many styles of stacking are there? To me, stack always meant one on top of the other."

"I'm a safety expert in this state."

Kyle heard the tarp crinkling.

"See there," said Swin. "Now we really need to haul ass."

This wouldn't be a huge deal, Kyle thought; they would pull the body in the cab and be on their way, then dump Bright in some field. The only trouble was the shot. Kyle and Swin could act confused and run back into the restaurant, asking if anyone knew where that shot came from. Then again, this was Texas. The diners might just look around for a moment, then continue stabbing their battered vegetables. This wouldn't be a big deal. It wasn't that complicated, was it? The biggest worry was that this ranger already knew what they were moving and was stalling until his backup showed. Shit, Kyle thought. Shit, here goes. Kyle stepped down from the cab with the gun showing. "Enough questions."

Bright laughed. "What are the cones for?" He held his palms up. "I'm with Frog. I've been ordered to intervene."

Bright told Kyle and Swin what they were carrying, where they'd left from and when, and that they had a map of each

JOHN BRANDON

state in the glove box. He explained that they had little choice about their immediate futures. They would work under Bright, at a park. Frog had cut a new loop of clients and Bright would run these deals. He'd known Frog for years, he told them, since he'd stopped one of his trucks lost in the park.

"Try not to look like deer in headlights," he told Kyle and Swin. "Look angry or bored or something."

Bright, Kyle, and Swin left the flatbed and the gun with someone in Austin and headed north toward the park in Bright's Bronco.

"I about blew you away," Kyle said.

Bright raised an eyebrow. "You trying to convince someone?"

"No, I hate guns. I'm saying it's not smart to fuck around with somebody you don't know."

Bright leaned around, looking at both boys in turn. "You're Kyle Ribb and you never killed a man. You're Swin Ruiz and you never killed a man. You're dependable, you're a project."

The air rushed thinly over Bright, who, guiding the Bronco up the highway with a thumb, felt a looming ease. He wouldn't have to do park labor. He'd hardly have to take trips anymore. He had a couple of charges who would long for his wisdom, who would pretend to ignore him but later, alone, would parse his words and file them away, shuffle and study them in bed at night. They could have family dinners. They could drink whiskey.

He turned to the boys and informed them they would have nine-to-five covers as park peons—maintaining the grounds, directing lost SUVs.

"We get paid for that, too?" Swin asked.

"The checks come to me and I burn them. Your names are Robert Suarez and Ed Mollar. I got you licenses and park IDs."

"We have to take out the garbage and shit?"

"Sure you do."

"I don't do well with a boss," Kyle said.

Swin leaned up between the seats. "I never had one."

"Everyone has a boss," Bright said.

"Frog probably has a boss."

"So you met Frog?"

"I spoke to a man on the phone that I believe was Frog."

"What led you to believe that?" asked Swin.

"He said 'This is Frog' before he started talking."

Bright's house had once been a school for woodworking. It had a huge main area and three yellow, bare bedrooms. Swin and Kyle wouldn't be staying with Bright. They would have matching trailers on the other side of the park. They would each keep two bags under their beds, one for their clothes and one for what-have-you.

For their cars, which would be sold, each would get five thousand dollars.

In the big room of Bright's house was a white TV, a cabinet stocked with plastic bottles of bourbon, and scattered tables loaded with books about nature. Bright chose a bottle and fetched three short glasses. He filled one and handed it to Swin, who set it down on a book of essays about the boilerplate rhino.

"I don't really drink," Swin said.

"You don't, huh? You're a strange one, aren't you, Swin? You fancy yourself a genius?"

"Genius is a bit much. I could've been an intellectual, though."

"Intellectuals are white and they don't work out."

"They jog," said Swin.

"When you first meet someone and he offers you a drink, you damn well drink it."

"Not trying to be a dick."

"I have a feeling that's your line," said Bright. "Mine is, 'May you dream of offered tits.' I say that once in a while."

Swin picked up his glass and brought it to his face. "Nope. I can't."

Bright handed each of them a key, a map of the park, a handbook for state employees, and a pamphlet on national wildlife reserves. "You two go cuddle up with these. And may you dream of offered tits."

The sun was high by the time Swin neared Bright's house the next morning. Kyle sat on the porch with a mug.

"You look like those guys on the do-it-yourself show," Swin said.

"Do *what* yourself?"

"You know, grout. Too bad it's summer; you could wear a nice turtleneck sweater."

Kyle stretched his legs and set down his mug. "You got quite an interest in my appearance." The coffee cup read THIS *IS* MY GOOD MOOD. "You're giving me that good-natured ribbing, right?"

"Now you do it back."

"It feels like flirting."

"It's very much like that."

Kyle's eyebrows spread. "Plenty of coffee," he said, gruffly.

"None for me. Makes me bored."

"Caffeine makes you bored?"

"Mugs and steam do. Just watching you drink that brings a malaise. Where's the boss?"

"Vacuuming."

Now Swin heard it. The noise had been blending with countless birds and rustlings and sways.

"You think there's any chance Bright *is* Frog?" Kyle asked.

"None," said Swin. "It's fresh thinking, though. An original yet dumb thought."

"Where do you think Frog lives?"

"You mean, what city?"

"You think he lives out on a ranch somewhere?"

"You don't get to be a crime boss by being solitary and contemplative; you get to be a crime boss by double-crossing and

JOHN BRANDON

scheming and inheriting, just like on Wall Street."

"I don't believe you know much about crime bosses *or* Wall Street."

"Not firsthand."

"The guy must have *something* figured out, to go that long without getting caught or killed."

Swin scratched the back of his neck. "We'll have to work in this company for a long time before we find out anything true about Frog."

"I heard he has a pool shaped like a lily pad."

"That's what I mean. For a long time, we'll only know things like that—inconsequential falsehoods."

They waited until the vacuum shut off and went in. Bright began putting away dishes.

"Sleep well? All nested in?" Bright paused, a pair of tongs in hand. "Would either of you like to call me sir?"

They looked at him.

"Because you can if you like. I won't think it's corny."

Bright kept unloading until the drainer was empty, then sat down at the dining room table, which held a stack of newsletters about bobcats.

"Your first trip is Florida," he said. "I think the Panhandle. This weekend." He picked his eye.

That afternoon, Kyle repainted the yellow

lines of the parking area. This took patience he did not have. He had to get down on his knees and drag the brush impossibly slowly with two hands. Before he put the paint down, he had to sweep each line. Twigs and leaves kept blowing into the wet paint. He dropped the brush a few times. His can ran dry and he had to walk back over by Bright's house and lug over another one.

As soon as he got into a rhythm with it, a middle-aged guy in an unbuttoned shirt started talking to him about an endangered toad, asking where he could get a glimpse of one.

"The far end of the pond." Kyle pointed with no conviction.

"I thought they didn't like water," the guy said.

"Not usually," said Kyle. "They've been acting confused."

"I heard they come out when the scrub laurels bloom."

"Yeah, they love those."

"When do they bloom?"

"Any time now."

When Bright's dinner was almost ready, he started complaining that he had no radishes for garnish, so Swin volunteered to hit the grocery. He wasn't about to eat whatever pork and squash concoction Bright kept sniffing. That big pot of food reminded him of his mother, who used to freeze tons of runny casserole. Swin and his sisters would choke down the nuked mush while Swin's father ate a pressed Cuban twice a day. Swin's father, when Swin's mother left the house, would heat up all the casserole portions at once and call the neighborhood kids over. He'd line them up single file and slap a clod on each one's plate, calling the kids the wrong names. The guy did everything slowly, as if nothing was worth getting excited about. The only thing that pleased him was watching the Gulf. The beach was the same for Swin's father as it was for the millionaire condo-owners—same glare, same shells breaking again and again in the surf. Swin used to sit with him while he smoked his cigars to nubs. He'd never once felt close to the man, never accepted a puff or found a way to impress him. Kyle, Swin knew,

would eat Bright's food and drink his liquor and become the darling.

The open-air grocery was crowded with barrels of nuts and peppers. Swin eyed a black-haired nurse with a fake tan while she filled a bag with chestnuts. The nurse wore blue scrubs and thick glasses. Something about her full bottom lip made Swin believe she must dig sex. She cracked two nuts together and put them in her mouth, and Swin went over and asked if she knew where radishes were. She located Swin's forehead through her bottle lenses and swallowed.

"With the vegetables? That's an educated guess."

Swin leered as if she'd said something naughty. "New in town," he said. "Name's Swin."

"Your name's about as dumb as mine: Johnna."

Swin conspicuously looked this nurse named Johnna from sneakers to barrettes. She had big yet uncrowded teeth and polka dots of blue polish on her nails. Her high breasts barely tented the front of her scrub shirt.

"There's no telling how long I'll be in the area," Swin said. He leaned against a barrel of fragrant chilis. "I'm a freelance government auditor."

Johnna was blushing through the brown of her cheeks, which created the effect of a blown disguise. She adjusted her glasses.

Swin said, "Let's get this courtship under way."

"I'm on shift tonight."

"Tomorrow night."

"Church."

"I'm out of town this—church?"

"You should try it."

"I have," Swin said. "We all have."

They agreed to meet for lunch on Thursday, right before Swin's departure for Florida. Johnna touched Swin's elbow and squeezed past him, maneuvering her hips through the barrels toward the checkout. Swin stepped into the produce room for the radishes. When he returned, Johnna was hissing at the clerk, a hairy individual with a thin neck. She ran down a list of his failures in life, which included community college, carpentry, and a run at the county board. Swin hoped she'd never had sex with this overall-draped dude. He wasn't fighting back. He totaled her order and made change. Johnna put the bills in her back pocket and told the clerk to feel free to die. Swin was convinced this woman had profound appetites. He slipped the radishes in his pocket and followed her outside. At her car, she turned on him with a stern look.

"What's with all the little muscles?"

"I stay ready to perform."

"It's creepy. The radishes and the tight shirt and the Duracell tattoos."

"Do you like creepy?"

Johnna unlocked her door and Swin opened it for her, ushering her with his arm. She started her car with much gunning of the engine, then traded out her glasses for a pair with tinted lenses. "You can't so much as kiss me for five dates."

"Then what?" Swin asked.

"Then you can."

Kyle and Swin drove a brown Volvo to Florida. They didn't know what they were hauling or where on the car it was hidden. Kyle took the first driving shift and Swin slept for five hours while Kyle chugged the unwieldy wagon down Interstate 10, stickers for sappy rock bands and politics all over his bumper. There was no notable change in the surroundings until Pensacola, where every building had a deck and the air stank of burning tires. Swin awoke and demanded they stop in Panama City for dinner. He assured Kyle that the one-time Panhandle backwater had surpassed Daytona as the beach party capital of Florida.

Low, spiky palms. Neon. Gift shops giving away three T-shirts for five dollars. Kyle and Swin ate in a shotgun building with sand on the floor, a place that offered endless beers from California and turned muggy any breeze that passed into it. They walked up the strip asking about wet T-shirt contests and got only chuckles and stares. Where were the women? Kyle asked. A dude wearing boots with shorts? What were those three guys doing?

Kyle and Swin gathered that something gay was happening in Panama City. Swin cornered an older man who seemed the same beige race as himself and found that they'd wandered into a convention of elderly homosexuals. Every man in sight—fat, foreign, disabled—was gay. Swin asked if Kyle wanted to hold hands. Kyle, sick of Swin's joking, reached down and seized Swin's nuts, causing him to backpedal and stumble over a curb. They stared at each other a long moment. Kyle, satisfied, extended his hand to Swin, who looked at it skeptically before taking it. Swin had scraped his arm and gotten his pants dirty. He put on his best smirk, took a couple peppy steps.

"I'm surprised your hand fit around those boulders," he said. "You're lucky you didn't break your fingers on those cannonballs."

"Always with the jokes," Kyle said. "Jokes, jokes."

"What's really lucky is that the old skin

cannon didn't go off." Swin's ego was almost fully intact again, that quickly, snapped back like elastic. "People have been maimed."

Most of the land on Highway 19, covered with dry oak trees and vines, was being sold off in parcels of five to twenty acres. There were no streetlights. The later it got, the hotter. By ten p.m. Kyle and Swin were running the air full blast and getting headaches from the bit of beer they'd drunk. The Volvo labored. They stopped at a gas station for high test and cold water and popped some Excedrin. Kyle said this state wasn't meant for white people and Swin answered that the whole country wasn't.

In Crystal River they passed a nuclear plant, then many signs shaped like manatees, some waving a flipper. Swin said the only two animals in the world with no natural defense were from Florida: manatees and love bugs. He detailed the accidental invention of love bugs, which were meant to be mosquito killers. Kyle told him that was fascinating and to get out the map and directions because they were close. They watched for a service station shaped like a dinosaur. They were in Hernando County. This newly populated stretch of the highway contained half a dozen strip clubs, one named Mom & Pop's. Kyle waited for Swin to suggest stopping at one so he could tell him no. The clubs had no signs, just names painted on the stucco.

"A place like that is where my sisters will end up." Swin tapped the window.

"How many of those you got? Ten?"

"Their titties are plumping this very minute."

"That tends to happen."

"They don't have their real father around and their stepdad is overly strict. Sounds like a stripper recipe to me."

Kyle used his T-shirt to mop his face. "You can never tell."

"Did you know that one in four women would agree to be abused if it meant they could eat anything and stay thin?"

"If they agree to it, it's not abuse."

"I mean they'd be willing to have it happen."

"Abused how?" Kyle asked.

"Does it matter?"

"It would to them."

They left the Volvo in the lot of the abandoned movie house, walked to a nearby Dunkin' Donuts to use a pay phone, then waited in an adjacent pine clearing. Kyle paced about and came upon a chainlink enclosure with two huskies inside. They didn't even bark at him. They panted a mile a minute and blinked their cloudy blue eyes, reclined pitifully on their sides as if shot. Kyle put a stick through the fence and pulled over the empty water bowl, then went into Dunkin' Donuts and got several cups of ice, which he carried out and poured in the bowl. The dogs rolled their heads and stared at Kyle, not understanding.

Soon a dump truck full of pineapple palms bumped into the lot. The driver got out and, as he'd said he would, began smoking two cigarettes. Kyle and Swin shouldered their bags and emerged from the pines.

The chores at the park were not usually taxing, but they were very boring. Kyle and Swin took turns sitting in the booth, wearing brown shirts with embroidered badges, collecting day-use fees of three dollars per car and handing out maps and pamphlets. The garbage cans on the grounds would've taken weeks to get full, but had to be emptied daily because of the critters. Kyle did some raking and weed-whacking and Swin put out birdseed. Bright opened the gate in the morning and Kyle was responsible for locking it at night. Swin went for jogs along the park boundary, avoiding being in his trailer, and this gave him occasion to run off a teenager or two, kids sneaking a can of beer or letting off bottle rockets. One day a kid in a tweed blazer was wandering around with a fishing net, nowhere near the pond. Swin yelled at him and the kid looked at Swin like he was a Martian and began holding forth about nude beaches. He'd been on a family vacation somewhere and had come back disillusioned. He described the world as a prude masquerade.

"I'm on something," the kid explained. "Something my brother brought back."

* * *

Johnna was pawning a scooter with a wooden body that she'd found abandoned near a railroad crossing. The pawnshop was a cement-block building that rested at the bottom of a muddy hill. There was no way to tell if the place was open. Johnna told Swin to make noise getting out of the car, so he slammed his door and loosed a yawn. He didn't know if Johnna was counting this as a date, but he was. He banged the scooter, which had no seat and was painted all over with bumblebees, up the stairs onto the porch, where Johnna rattled the screen door. Soon a man in a ball cap stepped into the doorway. The man said he was barbecuing shrimp, making dinner for breakfast. Johnna said she wasn't hungry. She pulled the scooter inside, then leaned it on her leg and touched it here and there, like someone showing a dog. The room was crowded with poetry books and packages of socks.

"A hundred," Johnna stated.

The man removed his cap and looked inside it. "Does it run?"

"You don't ride it. Thing's a curiosity."

"But it's wooden."

"Which is curious, right?"

"I guess it is."

"What if you *had* to buy it?"

"In that case, I'd give you fifty and sell it for eighty."

Swin raised a finger. "You're able to turn a profit with books and socks?"

"I don't have to turn a profit."

Johnna huffed. "This sucker's hand-painted."

"The bees don't look real. They're smiling."

"This scooter is a piece of America."

"I don't care about America. I care about listening to the St. Louis Cardinals on the radio." He checked his watch and was startled by what it said. He left the room.

Johnna was stoic behind her glasses. She explained that this man had moved to the area several years before with enough money to open a shop, fill it with useless shit like books, and never make a transaction. All he did was cook breakfast and listen to the radio. He was mean. With all that money, he wouldn't give you ten bucks for a Rolex.

He came back with a plastic-wrap-covered plate of sticky shrimp.

"I'm sorry, dear," he said. "You two can take some poetry with you."

Johnna sighed. "Tell you what I need is a saw. Handsaw."

"Just a minute."

The man left the room once again. Johnna rolled the scooter onto the porch and Swin followed with the shrimp. The air was hot and crowding. Swin told Johnna that if she needed money, he had some. She shook her head, said she simply wanted to be able to sell something she'd found, to rightly trade an interesting object for U.S. currency.

When the man returned with the saw Johnna let the scooter tip over, sat Indian-style beside it, and went to work on the handlebars, savagely yanking, a layer of sawdust forming on the porch floor, a droplet of sweat clinging to her glasses. Despite her strain, she wasn't cutting through the wood. Swin and the man looked at one another and the man winked. For a moment, Swin thought the man knew what he was thinking, that Johnna's current hotness and frustration were indicative of other hotnesses and frustrations, and that she was looking forward to their fifth date as much as he was.

The next trip was short. Kyle and Swin were to cross into Louisiana, barely into the swamps, and drop off a net bag of soccer balls filled with pills. They drove a Ford Taurus with digital dash meters and a CD player for which they'd brought no CDs. Kyle was sick of words, even his own.

"No more radio," he said.

"There's a lot of good stations around here," said Swin. "This is a musical area."

"Not today it isn't."

Swin picked at his door handle, a nuisanced look on his face. "What, are you going to contemplate the nature of the ever-expanding universe and man's place in it?"

"Doubt it. But if I do have a thought, I'll hear it."

"Sure," Swin said. "*If* you have one."

"I feel one coming on."

"Maybe you should pull off."

"Nope. Nope, false alarm."

"So now let's turn the old radio back on."

"Tell you what," Kyle said. "Find something with no words in it."

"But I'm in the mood for blues. I want to hear that one where the guy says it's nobody's business if he wakes up crazy and kills his baby."

"Take a nap."

"Hey! Welcome to Louisiana."

Kyle checked his watch.

"You ever been to Mardi Gras?" Swin asked.

"I'm not sure."

Many towns whizzed past. Lots of churches. Lots of food stands. A black man with no shoes holding something that was on fire.

* * *

They pulled up to the trailer and honked four times. The door cracked open and an arm waved them in. Kyle lugged the balls in like Santa Claus, and a swarthy guy in slippers cut the bag open and began puncturing the underinflated spheres one by one, his knife tearing through the glossy vinyl.

"In my country," he said, "is rude not to study something you buy. You like Capri Sun?"

Swin said, "Sure."

"We buy bulk. We're sick of them. Poking that straw is an American stupidity. The juice, it squirts out."

"We?" said Kyle.

The man stopped tearing up the soccer balls. "My nephew." He called the name Nick. "Bring juice pouch this minute."

A kid about high-school age appeared and tossed Swin a Capri Sun. The kid shook his head, as if daunted by the thought of getting rid of all the Capri Sun in his stewardship. He had close-set eyes and slicked hair, like an old-fashioned immigrant. As he left the room, he grunted something in Greek that caused his uncle to fly off the sofa, knife still in hand. Kyle stood and said, "Easy." The man looked at the weapon in his hand.

"Look how rude. I wave this thing. Nick, speak English in front of friends. You know only curses, anyway. Let them see you or they get nervous. They don't know how harmless you are."

Nick doubled back into the room, leaned on the wall, and began messing with the wristbands he wore on each forearm. Kyle told the uncle not to worry so much about being rude, but instead to hurry up and check the balls and bring out the money. This main room of the trailer contained a sofa, on which the uncle sat, two folding chairs, on which Swin and Kyle sat, several mason jars of pennies, and a stack of license plates. The floor was scattered with slippers.

"His poor papa drove a tow truck," the uncle said. "The least noble profession of the world. Even police are sometimes noble. Or teachers or singers. Not tow-truck drivers."

Nick shook his head. His uncle broke a pill open and dumped it in an ashtray. Using a turkey baster, he doused it with a pink liquid.

"His papa told me what great comfort it was he could kill himself. When life was hard, he thought of this. A strange egg, as Americans say. As a child he paid another boy to partake in the carnal act with a dog. Small dog."

"Dogs enjoy sex with humans," Swin said. "It would be like you having sex with a super-hot alien."

Now Nick smiled. Maybe he was slow. Swin held up his empty Capri Sun and Nick took it from him and disappeared. The uncle had two balls left. He sighed, put the knife in a drawer, and brought out a different one.

"What county of Arkansas are you from?"

"Tell him to bring in the money," Kyle said.

"Sorry, rude question. All these customs."

"Don't say the word 'rude' again. It's in my power to pull the deal."

The guy yelled for his nephew to bring in the bag.

"My plight is horrible one," he said. "I only ask what county because I once designed water towers. Fifty-one towers for Alabama, Mississippi, Arkansas. Now the fashion changes. No new towers. Now I'm not noble. Now I am threatened by men in my home."

Kyle nodded. "Could be worse. If he doesn't get that bag out here in a hurry, it could get worse."

The man called out again and Nick came in with the bag and gave it to Swin, who opened it and took a look. Nick's grin was amused. He wasn't slow. In fact, something about him was condescending. As Kyle and Swin left the trailer, the uncle said, "No hard feelings."

Kyle replied, "No feelings at all."

Swin drove. Kyle reclined his seat and wondered about Nick, about why someone would subject themselves to such shit. It was only a matter of time, Kyle thought, before that kid offed his uncle and ate him. That head shaking was pure maniac. Swin said whoever was driving made the rules about the radio, then tuned in a folk station that was begging for donations. Kyle wondered about the nation of Greece, about the field of water-tower design, about what it would be like to have an uncle. He drifted and had a dream in which he tried to relax in a breezy place. A resort. He didn't know the name of the drink he wanted to buy for an older woman.

It was not easy for Nick to follow the Taurus in a Datsun hatchback with an 85-horsepower engine. Several times, he had to scream his roller skate of an automobile and close in on the Taurus to see the stuffed Razorback in the rear window, wearing a #4 jersey. If these two dudes from Arkansas knew he was trailing them, they weren't going to let on. The blinkers of the Taurus flashed only when the car moved from right to left, and its speed was sporadic. Nick was burning up, his insides cramping. He calmed himself with the thought of having enough money to move somewhere rugged where he would get a certificate to be an X-ray tech, keep a clean trailer, and head down to the bar once a week with fresh fingernails. People would say he was a regular dude—run-of-the-mill, good dude. Nick didn't know why he hadn't been able to kill his uncle before he left. He suspected his uncle had some kind of slave grip on his mind. The guy had told everyone in their town that Nick was lazy and stole, preventing him from getting a job at the mug factory or the outfit where they put ketchup and mustard in packets. He talked Nick's father down at every turn, though Nick's father had supported him for years while he was out of work, before he found his way into the drug trade. For a solid year, until he got bored with it, Nick's uncle had called Nick "Prickolas." Nick wasn't quite eighteen. His uncle had reminded him every day that if he left he'd be reported missing, tracked down, and dragged back in disgrace. On this outing, though, Nick would have the means to get as far away as his Datsun would take him. By the time anyone found him, he'd be the lawful owner of a nice adult life. Because of his maturity, folks would know he'd been through something. It was common knowledge that women liked a dude who'd been through something.

Two hours from home, Nick realized he'd never driven this far. He should've brought a tape player because the radio in his Datsun didn't work. A voice in his head sang bits of the song "Honesty" at a sped-up pace. How was the word "honesty" easy? Easy to spell? Easy to do? The rhythm of the song conformed to the bump and hum of the tires against the road, and Nick couldn't shake it. His face was sweating. He'd already rubbed his forehead raw against his wristbands. Deep breaths were what was called for. Nick wanted coffee. He hadn't drunk it since he was a kid, since his father gave him sips

from a metallic thermos. The Taurus was never going to stop for gas. It had settled in behind a semi in the right lane. Nick thought of his uncle's gun in the glove box. It was tarnished black and prone to kick down and left, but at short range it would get the job done. He imagined getting pulled over, having his gun confiscated, getting returned, in cuffs, to his uncle's trailer. He banished the thought that he'd be relieved.

The Taurus broke onto a two-lane county road and suddenly Nick wasn't anxious. He felt himself to be a natural detail of the place. Dawn was starting. Nick was surrounded by broken-top hills. The Taurus pulled into a park with a funny name and Nick parked outside the gate and killed his lights, tossed his sopping wristbands on the floor. He had a sixteenth of a tank of gas. He shut off the engine. He had a book bag that had been given to him by a charity which had also given him a set of rulers. He put his gun in the book bag, which already held a hammer and a tangle of thick shoelaces, and waited about five minutes, giving the dudes from the Taurus a chance to feel safe. Nick didn't know if they were going to camp in the park or if they had a meeting scheduled or what, but this park probably had only one entrance, so they wouldn't be able to leave without Nick knowing about it. He entered the park on foot and headed down a path blocked off by a gate with a sign that read PARK EMPLOYEES ONLY. He scaled a dry hill scarred with stump holes. From the top, he saw a Bronco and a low, expansive house. No sign of the Taurus. Lights on in the house. Nick descended the hill and hid behind the Bronco. He needed to observe, to find out what was waiting in there. An old lady with a bunch of sons? A Confederate militia? There was nothing inside the Bronco—no music or food containers or corny objects hanging from the rearview. There were, however, fresh tire tracks up the drive and back down, and a set of footprints to the porch and back. After about two minutes of observation, Nick felt like a sitting duck. He scaled the porch steps without creaking them and positioned himself outside the front door. TV. An announcer who was maybe Scottish was explaining the financial straits of some rugby league. As far as Nick could figure, the dudes in the Taurus had dropped something here, whether it was his uncle's money or something else of value. Nick would've rather had cash, but a good amount of drugs, if that's what it had to be, would work. When he went inside and encountered this dude, whether it was some thorny chief runner or pumped skinhead or just some loser like Nick's uncle, Nick wouldn't let on that he didn't know what he was looking for. He tried the door handle and the lever yielded to his thumb. He unzipped his book bag and removed the gun, pressed it against his thigh. He nudged the door open an inch, his body snug against it, and took

a moment to breathe—not stalling. He wasn't going to stall. He put his eye to the opening and saw part of a large room—books everywhere in uneven stacks, the television. Nick let the door open another foot and yanked himself inside. He was stopped short by the sight of a hulking cabinet stocked with dozens of identical liquor bottles, all half-empty. He shut the door behind him and slipped into the nearest room, weapon at the ready. The room was blank, yellow, with no closet and a fan in the corner. Nick peered down the long hall before taking the next room, also yellow, matching the other except that it held a shiny vacuum with countless accessories. The machine was like an injured animal, plug hanging half out of the socket, tubing draped about like maimed limbs. Nick was scared to turn his back on the thing. He paced farther down the hall and halted at the next open doorway. In the same glance, his eyes found the stack washer and dryer, trisection laundry basket, cardboard box full of light bulbs, lopsided hill of pamphlets, and the bald man down on one knee, holding a broom and dustpan. It took what felt like a long time for the man to transfer his attention from the floor to Nick and his pistol. When he did, his eyes lit up.

"I don't mean to die before I whip this dust."

Nick was out of his league, but the man didn't know that. Nick instructed him to empty his hands and remove his boots and socks. The man did this, yawning, then cracked his toes. Nick put him on his front and tied his wrists behind his back with shoelaces, led him to the first bedroom, the one with the fan, where the man got back down on his stomach without being told.

"Fetch a couple chairs from the kitchen," he said. "I ain't heading nowhere."

Nick got one chair from the kitchen, put the man in it, tied his ankles.

"Time is a consideration," the man said. "Go ahead and tell me what you want."

"I'll decide what's a consideration," Nick said. He pulled the hammer from his bag.

"I got seventy bucks in my wallet."

Nick swung the hammer at the man's abdomen, stepping into it, and though no jarring shock seized the handle, a loud crack was heard, the man's hip bone. The man sucked air through his teeth. Nick swung again, not aiming this time, and the hammer thudded into the flesh of the man's upper arm. This time, his grunt had a higher pitch.

"My name is Bright." His feet were shaking. "It's only decent I tell you, I'm a state employee."

"This hammer is a Craftsman. If I wear it out, I can trade it in for a new one."

Nick was impressed with himself. He went to the kitchen to brew coffee and found the maker already set up. All he had to do was flip it on and wait for the first drops to dink in the pot. Nick found a mug that read I HATE THE LONGHORNS FROM THE TIME I WAKE UP. He knew he couldn't indulge the situation too far. In the past minutes he'd found something he was good at, something that came to him. He felt smart. When the coffee maker quieted, he poured some. It was like sludge. He added a lot of milk and tasted the bitter stuff, dumped it in the sink and turned off the pot. At the far end of the hall he found the master bedroom, got a wire hanger from the closet, and straightened it. He strolled back into the room with Bright.

"I don't lie to folks in the business," Bright told him. "I'm expecting guests for breakfast."

"I can tell that's not true."

Bright was slumped in the chair now,

favoring his battered hip. He was focused but distant, like he wanted to fall asleep with his eyes open. "Done in by an adolescent," he said.

"When your father dies, you're no longer a kid."

"My father died young. I was happy about it, though."

"Well, I wasn't."

"Where you from, son? At least tell me that."

"Castor, Louisiana."

"Castor?"

"I followed the dudes in the Taurus."

"You followed them? Who was driving?"

"The shorter one."

"The beige one?"

Nick nodded.

"You two worked something out, huh? You worked something out with Swin, didn't you?"

"They didn't know about it."

"Don't bullshit me," Bright said. "Swin couldn't face me for the dirty work."

"This is *my* dirty work and I wouldn't do anybody else's."

"Kyle's over there snoring and Swin's lying in a pool of sweat, straining to hear a pop."

Nick paused. "They live in the park?"

"What's the state of things when a person like me can be disgusted?"

Nick felt it slipping away. Bright didn't seem hurt anymore. Nick had lost his mystery. He bent for the hammer and turned with a low, compact swing that shattered his captive's shin. Bright's body twitched from its core.

Nick waited for Bright to settle a bit, then he brandished the hanger.

"Don't you think Swin has the money if he's producing this picture?"

"I don't want to hear Swin or the other one's name one more time. I know you got a stash in this place and you're going to give it to me."

"So you can waste it on junior college? You wouldn't know what to do with my stash."

Nick wet one end of the hanger and palmed Bright's bald head like a volley-ball. He tapped around the inside of his earlobe with the hanger.

"You're not bluffing," Bright said.

"You figured that out?"

"I've never been tortured before."

Nick felt resistance and pressed the hanger in, causing Bright to gasp and jerk his head. The hanger tinked across the floor.

"Nowhere near the other side," Nick said.

"I've had enough. Jesus, I've had my fill. I'll give you what you want."

Nick hurried to the kitchen for a glass of water and dumped it on Bright's head. He asked where the money was and Bright's answer was ready: the attic. Inside an air duct. He could fish it out with one hand, but nobody else would be able to, even with instructions. About fifty grand.

In the hall, Nick pulled down the staircase and held Bright steady as he scaled it, wincing with each step on his wrecked leg. Nick then secured his gun in his waistband and climbed up and sat Bright down on a rafter. Nick was hunched over and could barely breathe the brittle air. On first glance, he saw no air duct. There was one light bulb and no windows. Bright told him to free his right hand and tie his left to his belt loop behind him, and to move a box of pink flyers and the terra cotta pots.

Nick saw his future, saw himself crossing leaning wheat fields, the Rockies coming into view, sunflowers behind him and snow ahead, stacks of hundred-dollar bills in his book bag. He leaned farther over and took Bright by the arm to turn him, and then they were stumbling. Nick felt a beam smack the back of his head. He landed on his ass, groped to get the gun from his waist. Bright managed a sideways lunge and his weight fell on Nick's legs. Nick squeezed the trigger, the gun kicking wildly. Bright was bleeding all over Nick's lower half. Another hand was on the gun. Bright's arms were loose, though one was pinned beneath him, and with his free hand he twisted the gun to crush Nick's fingers. Bright had the barrel. Nick wanted to catch him in the face with an elbow, but he was inches out of reach. The gun was wrenching Nick's fingers, breaking his will to hold on. He hoped his knuckles had a plan of their own, but no.

There was a second of relief when the steel slipped free, and then warmth coursed through Nick's shoulder. He wondered what he'd do next, was surprised to see his arms extended, pinning Bright's hand, the gun fast against the floor. Bright had fired twice. One bullet went into Nick and one bore a perfect circle in the roof, through which light poured in and rested on Bright's bald head.

"I always thought I'd die outdoors," Bright said. "I don't know why. Just a feeling."

"We're not dead."

"Oh, no?"

"We're okay."

"That's the rest of your life talking."

Nick kicked and tried to roll Bright off, but the two of them were wedged between rafters on a bed of insulation. Their blood was mixing. It felt to Nick like he was pissing his pants. He couldn't feel his arm, couldn't feel anything but his heart, which kept forcing its red leak. Maybe Bright would die first. Nick waited. He watched the blue hole full of light. He grew comfortable with the itching, dozed off. At least an hour passed. Bright's eyes were shut but he was still breathing and was still intent on his death grip. It seemed he was going to speak. Nick resolved not to answer him. Bright opened his eyes long enough to find Nick's and mumbled something about dreaming of tits.

JOHN BRANDON

BEACHHEAD, *by Sgt. Irwin S. Caplan (Ft. Knox, Ky.)*

SLEEP

For information on the Amanda Davis High-wire Fiction Award, please see the back cover of this issue's book of New Stories from Overseas.

I bought my bed from a dead girl. She was alive when I bought it, but inside ticking like a bomb. She must have known she had only a little life left, must have felt small parts of her leaking away. That's why she sold the bed for such a small price. At the time I thought it was desperation, but now I think it was a gamble: cast off the grand, comfortable things of life faster than your body casts off its future and maybe you'll win more time.

She was selling all her things piece by piece. Flinging each piece of earthliness into the arms of someone else. The price for the bed was insultingly low, cheaper than when she'd first mentioned it, months before. But she called me on a September Monday and said, "If you want it it's yours."

"I want to travel," she told me over the phone. "I'm leaving New York. There are places I've never been, and I'm off to check them out."

So I brought my superintendent with me, through the navy yard and into the

written by Amanda Davis

quiet streets under the Manhattan Bridge in my rumbly, battered red van. Andrew wanted to marry me, had offered me $3,000 to make him an American, but I couldn't stomach his bar fighting, his fetid moustache, his habit of extreme inebriation. I was interested only in his ability to fix things, and his brute strength.

We found her loft. She was waiting outside on the steps, sun on her face. We said hello. I did not know her well. She was thinner than I remembered, and shy, but her expression was kind.

Andrew and I climbed the stairs to an enormous empty space. She showed us where to go and watched us wrestle her mattress and box spring to the street.

They refused to fit inside my van but she was undeterred, unshaken. She smiled. "I have something," she said, and bounded back up the stairs.

See, this is the way with misremembering. How could she bound when a few months later she was dead: her diseased body stiffened to stone from the inside out? On that particular day, she must have been crumbling slowly, her body beginning its betrayal. How could she leap? She must have creaked up the stairs, every effort to conceal her woodenness lost on us: two wrestlers of a mattress, laughing in the fine, light day.

Had I known her body was hardening, I might remember more. But how would we have helped her?

I don't remember how much time

passed before she returned, five minutes or one or ten. I rummaged through my van and giggled with Andrew at the impractical things we found there: old bags, a stray shoe, shards of glass, a trumpet. Products of my messiness and whimsy, but nothing to restrain a mattress, a box spring.

And then she reappeared. "Here," she said, slightly out of breath. We took the packing tape she offered, and began to wrap and wrap, binding her bed to my van.

She stood in front of her building for a moment while I thanked her. I remember she seemed frail, tiny. A timid adventurer preparing for travels, an exhausted twenty-two-year-old preparing to move, to go exploring. In the glaring, late-afternoon sun she waved goodbye, then turned—the last time I saw her—and slowly started up the stairs. And I remember her shoulder blades beating sharply beneath her shirt.

We departed then, each with a hand out the window, holding her bed to my roof, convinced our firm touch could persuade it to stay.

She died two months later, suddenly, not so suddenly. Her disease had been with her a long time, but to those of us not close enough to know it, her departure was an unexpected subtraction. A disappearance, not a slipping away.

I still think of her when I change the sheets. For a while I lay awake at night in the hollow her body left. For a time I wondered if her dreams had survived, seeped into the fibers, leaking into mine.

CONVOY THROUGH ORBATELLO, *by Waldo Bogart (Woodrow Wilson Gen. Hosp., Va.)*

CHARITY

Vic's new mechanic arrived that morning from the sodden rubble of New Orleans. As he watched him climb out of a little beater Chevette, Vic felt a pang of employer's remorse. Royce was heavily tattooed and jacked with muscle, his arms sloped out, wrists hovering inches from his waist. His sandy red hair was gelled straight up on top like standing flames. But he talked in gentle Southern and averted his eyes in shame when asked about his prison record. "Methamphetamines," he said. "I opened the front door of hell itself."

Vic, who turned fifty that year, happened to be looking back on a decade of selfish living when Royce's caseworker called. She had read Vic's classified ad online. Royce was hardworking and personable, she said, as strong a candidate as he could hope to find. Her urgency roused images of the news he'd watched all week, evacuees baking on shadeless sidewalks, T-shirts waving like white flags from the water-lapped roofs of houses. Vic found himself compelled by the idea of charity. Otherwise, he never would have shelved a stack of solid applications for the faxed

written by Wayne Harrison

résumé of a man he hadn't met.

In the shop bays Vic introduced his other mechanics with short accolades. Mike Lorenzo had worked on Jeff Gordon's pit crew. Last year Eddie Cobb patented a carburetor-adjusting tool he optioned to Snap-on. Felix Diaz was the youngest ASE-certified master mechanic in Oregon.

"Damn," Royce said, shaking hands. "Y'all sound like some kinda dream team."

"Let me see them tats," Eddie said.

Royce smiled uneasily and pulled up his shirt. Vic saw axes, flowers, names, words: *Ice Man. Unchained.* He was like a piece of mail that had been everywhere. Eddie and Felix looked, then showed their own. Checkered flag. Barbed wire. Cougar head. *Wrap Your Ass in Fiberglass*, written around a Corvette. Caught up in their fellowship, Vic raised his own sleeve to the shoulder. From a stint in the army he had a narrow, rippling flag. "Old Glory," he said, feeling sincere with his kids—he thought of them that way. "That's all a man needs."

Later in the morning Mike Lorenzo tapped the open door to Vic's office on his way in. Vic had been trying to finish a parts order for nearly an hour, memories of his own agonizing trek to Oregon breaking his concentration. Royce was staying with his sister and didn't need an apartment, but Vic had started a list of tool distributors, Sears and Safeway locations, things he'd need to know. He looked up at Mike. "How's he doing?"

"I got him putting in a water pump on

that El Camino. So far so good." Mike sat and picked at a callus on his palm. "He say why he was in the clink down there?"

"First thing out of his mouth."

Mike watched him and sat further back in the chair. He had a black handlebar moustache that intensified even his calm expressions. After nine years here, Mike was owed full disclosure, but Vic was feeling superstitious. It seemed like a delicate fate that had put Royce in his hands.

Vic leaned over his papers and spoke calmly. "Eddie came to me on parole, and he's working out. Let's give the guy a clean slate."

Mike laughed through his nose with some disgust. He reached for an oil additive display on Vic's desk. In it three gears aligned vertically: he cranked a steel handle around and around, bringing the tan fluid to the top. He stood from the chair and turned for the door. "Long as tools don't go missing," he said.

That evening Vic stopped at a basement jazz club near the university. It was his usual place to pass the long hour before dinner at home with CNN. At the smallest booth in back he sat and mused over three pints of beer.

In Connecticut his marriage had ended brutally. He and Carolyn lied routinely and demeaned each other, and when she started fooling around he sold their Pepsi stock—a wedding gift from his parents—and left town. She had always wanted to move cross-country to Oregon.

He pushed on from state to state until, drunk outside Lincoln, Nebraska, he decided that living her dream would be the best way to punish her.

Last year he'd received a short, loveless letter from his daughter Amanda. She had given birth to a baby girl of her own. There was no mention of the father, and the return address was an apartment number in a town some ways south of where Carolyn and her new husband were living. The envelope held two photographs of his granddaughter in her mother's arms. That one was a wallet-size touched him. He hadn't spoken to Amanda in three years, since a phone call she'd cut off with fuck-filled teenage insults he couldn't listen to.

He framed the larger print and kept it in the living room over his TV. He sent a check for a thousand dollars in a congratulations card he signed *Love Dad*.

Royce's son came up by Greyhound as soon as Royce was settled. A freckly, red-haired seven-year-old, Sam became an afternoon fixture in the lobby, where he did his reading and workbook assignments after school. In the evenings, his homework done, Sam would ask customers politely—sir or ma'am—if he could turn on cartoons. Vic remembered the ones he'd watched with Amanda: *Looney Tunes*, *Care Bears*, shows where animals ran the world. Now they were all people with big eyes flying around blasting lasers through outer space.

Some days Sam came behind the counter and helped Vic prepare bank deposits. Money excited him, and Vic showed him how to check twenties with iodine pens, where the states were written across the Lincoln Memorial Building on old five-dollar bills.

One night in particular convinced Vic that Sam and his father were fitting in. They were all in the lobby after work watching the Englishtown quarter-mile races on TV. Vic sipped his cream stout, Mike his porter, Eddie and Felix their amber ales. Leaned over his knees watching the races, Royce pulled from a bottle of near beer.

Eddie was telling a story about friends who'd come to fighting in a bar. He could barely finish for laughing. He held up his flat hand near his face and with the other hand punched it again and again. "Bam," he said. "Bam, bam. And that Morgan. I mean, he won't go down. Bam." He laughed his high, windy laugh. "Bam, bam. Gore running out his nose. Out his eyebrow. The dude's so completely annihilated, just fucked-up drunk—"

"Eddie, can the language," Vic said. "The kid."

Eddie wiped his eye and nodded. "Sorry, little man," he said. Adding numbers on the calculator, Sam bumped Vic with his knee. "That don't bother me," the boy said.

Vic bumped him back. "It ought to."

"What's worse for cussing, Boo?" Royce said. "Around here or Aunt Suzi's cable?"

"Cable," Sam said.

"There's no getting around it," Royce said, then shook his head. "These kids today seen every manner of sin before kindergarten."

On television a Hemi Cuda paired up against a Cobra Jet Mustang. The start light fell from amber to green, and eight seconds later the Cuda crossed the line at 170 miles per hour.

"Arrest that boy!" Royce said, turning from the TV. "Y'all run quarter miles up here?"

"On pump gas or giggle gas?" Felix said, and Eddie interrupted: "I ran high twelves in my old Formula."

"The hell you say."

"Me and my uncle ran eleven-four at one eighteen in his El Camino," Felix said.

"Cam, headers, and glass packs. Stock otherwise."

"God and little fishes."

Even Mike told about his '68 Hemi Challenger running low tens, a car in which Mike's best friend had hit a bridge abutment and died violently. Vic watched them talk. Like family around a dinner table, he thought.

OCTOBER

Mornings in the locker room Royce brought his sleepy, staring, reticent coworkers to life with stories from the haunted bayous. Pulling on coveralls he talked of his grandmother's superstitions, of always leaving a house through the door you entered, of never borrowing salt, of staring at the point of a knife blade to cure hiccups. He had a wart on his finger he rubbed with a raw potato. "Where y'at?" he'd say when he came in, having taught them all the proper Cajun response: "Ah-rite."

Business was good. With a big-block Camaro fetching sixty thousand dollars, the shop catered to a new breed of hot-rodders who didn't know Vise-Grips from Channel Locks, but who had the bankrolls to medicate their midlife trauma with horsepower. Royce sold them engine chrome and beefed-up exhaust, increased displacement or more carburetion, often doubling the written estimates. In the lobby they shelled it out happily, as though he'd just done them an enormous favor.

It was his way of speaking, Vic thought, unhurried and ruminative, satisfied with the words he chose. He padded his explanations with "yessir" and "y'all," and his humor was always good-natured. "That Royce, he really explains it," the customers said at the register.

NOVEMBER

Sam came into the lobby one afternoon holding a small batch of sticks tied with shoelace, his jacket spattered with mud. Vic was explaining a valve job, and when the customer had gone he came around the counter and took the seat next to Sam.

"That a voodoo doll?"

"It's fixing to be."

"Not of me, I hope."

"No, sir. Billy Cornelius." Sam took off

his jacket and pulled the sleeve of his shirt up to the elbow, revealing a pink five-inch scratch. "He tripped me at the swings on purpose."

"How come he did that?"

"He said I talk like a shit-for-brains."

Vic sighed and looked out at the sky through the lobby windows. The clouds were runny with frayed edges where sunlight fell through. "This Cornelius kid," he said. "I bet he gets picked on at home. One thing about bullies is they always have it worse than you do."

Vic asked to see the doll, which resembled a person only in the vaguest sense. An alternative to violence, it seemed like the best idea in the world. He handed it back. "Who taught you that?"

"My momma. She can do nice ones." When Sam looked up from the doll his face pinched. Like water sloshed from a cup, the tears ran down to his lips. All he could say was that she was nice. She was so nice.

Vic stood and went to pour a bit of the hot water they set out for tea into a Styrofoam cup. "Follow me," he said, and led the boy back to his office. They sat together on the old sofa. Vic dipped the bottom half of the doll, where the feet and waist would be, into the water. He had a small refrigerator in the corner, and when he set the sticks in the freezer box on top Sam laughed wickedly.

Over roach-coach lunches the next day Vic asked Royce about Sam's mother. They were in the parts room, just the two of them. "We was Adam and Eve in the garden until this old girlfriend tracked me down," he said. "I like to hanged myself when Maggie found out."

The story wasn't surprising. Happiness excited desires, and suddenly you were tempted by the next thing. With his eager Huck Finn expressions, Royce made cheating and meth arrests sound unavoidable.

"I was a silver-lipped operator of bullshit," Royce said. "Nothing got through this thick old head." He opened his hands on his knees and looked at Vic. "Man, you got a cigarette?"

Vic handed him his pack and lighter. "Didn't know you smoked."

"On and off since the age of nine." Royce drew on the cigarette until the tip blinked yellow. "Maggie," he said, lifting his pale eyes, likely seeing her in his mind. "She was too good for me, was the problem." He dragged again and held the smoke deep inside.

DECEMBER

Royce overhauled his first engine, a '70 Le Mans 350, a week before Christmas. Vic had been watching him covertly, so that Royce wouldn't feel nervous or untrusted, through the lobby window. Aside from the engine removal and installation points that demanded two people, the guys respectfully left him alone. Vic was hanging up a work order on the pegs as Royce tightened the last carburetor bolt. Royce double-checked the firing order, the rotor position with the timing mark on top dead center, and then filled the radiator with antifreeze. Then he stood in front of the grille, glancing from point to point. Vic walked over and patted him on the shoulder. "Go on, son. Fire it up."

Royce waved for Sam to come out from the lobby.

"You did it, Dad?" the boy said.

"I think I just might of," Royce said. He opened the driver's door. "Maybe you better turn the key, Boo. I don't have the guts."

The engine caught on its third spin, and Vic listened with his eyes closed for misfiring. After a minute watching the gauges with Sam on his lap, Royce got out and came around to the fender.

"Oil pressure's good?" Vic said.

"Good and high."

"Bring her up," Vic said. Royce opened the throttle, the wind of the fan pushing his hair back. The engine revved smoothly and he smiled as though in a tropical breeze. Sam hugged him from behind. "That's *sweet*, Dad," he said, and then there was applause from Felix and Eddie.

In a few minutes Mike came out from the lobby with the cordless phone. He handed it to Royce. "A lady for you. She said your sister told her to call here."

"Jesus." Royce mashed his hand against the receiver. "It's Maggie?"

"She didn't give her name."

Sam jumped in place and called out "Mom!" until Royce told him to pipe down.

"You know, that's probably long distance," Vic said.

Royce took the receiver into the parts room and Sam stayed with Vic. Sam had thirty dollars from Vic's pay for sweeping the bays and was waiting for the Snap-on tool man who came on Fridays. He had his first screwdriver set all picked out.

"I knew she'd call," Sam said, folding and unfolding his five-dollar bills. "I asked for it in my prayers."

When the big white Snap-on van pulled in and parked, Sam, who'd been waiting all week, didn't even notice. "Look who's here," Vic said. Sam stared outside and then at the closed door of the parts room. When Royce finally came back, Sam had just gone out to buy his screwdrivers.

Royce set the phone down on two cases of GOJO, then stared at it like a man in shock. Vic was torn. His head told him to mind his own business. "What'd she say?" he asked.

Royce looked up and blinked. "That she misses us."

"You and Sam?"

"Sure enough. She's telling me about her job and how it is after rehab, and all the while, I'm saying to myself, All right, boy, you better step on up to that plate. But I couldn't get myself talking."

"She going to call again?"

"I don't know. I hope." He picked up the paperwork for the Pontiac. After a few moments of squinting like it was all in Greek, he set the clipboard on a tool tray.

"I can't even remember how many hours this job took me," he said.

The next morning Vic called Royce's caseworker and asked about Maggie. He mentioned possibly bussing her up to Oregon for a visit.

"What do you know about methamphetamines?" Devona said. The gravity of her tone made Vic realize he knew little. On the news he'd seen west-end houses raided, the bloodshot, emaciated addicts rounded up out of the shadows like vampires.

"But she finished her rehab. And Royce is clean from day one up here."

"It doesn't make them good for each other."

The phone in the crook of his neck, Vic stared down at a legal pad on which he'd written MAGGIE in block letters. "You think she could get him started again?"

"Or the other way around. Or nothing could happen, I don't know. I have babies outside my door with missing parents, and you want me to worry about this?"

"I can cover the cost of getting her out here," Vic told Royce. A week had passed since the first phone call from Maggie. "I don't mind."

"How long would she stay?"

"You two could talk about that. As long as you wanted."

Royce wiped his forehead with his sleeve.

He walked away from Vic, over to the bay windows, where he stared at the wet street colored by Broadway traffic lights. "You know what she said last night? That she wants to be enough for me this time. Isn't that something else? Her enough for me?"

"Sounds like she's thinking it through."

"It's great and hell at the same time." Royce came back smiling but shaking his head. "I prayed to God she'd come back when I'd be able to take care of her." Eyes glassed over, he looked at one of the words inked into his forearm. "I'd like to put some sandpaper to this goddamn skin of mine," he said.

JANUARY

On a drizzling northwest afternoon, Vic and Sam watched *Charlie and the Chocolate Factory* in Vic's office, the indigo TV light washed over the furniture. Sam was lying knees curled up on the sofa, his head on a throw pillow. The scene brought Vic back to a rented house in Hartford, his daughter beside him on a sofa, her plastic diaper crackling as she took raisins one at a time off his thigh.

"Your dad seems a little stressed out," Vic said.

"Him and Mom been talking a lot. Fighting sometimes."

"Fighting?"

Sam looked at him. "Naw, not *fighting* fighting. Like he says, 'Who's this crawdad cook you keep talking about? Well, I can't help if I am.' Meaning if he's jealous a little.

He just gets nervous." He looked back at the TV.

In the movie a fat kid slurped dark chocolate from a lake. Vic saw a tiny Mike in the miniature doorway reflected in the bottom of the screen. Vic could guess what he wanted, but he didn't turn. He patted the boy's foot. "What's the word on Billy Cornelius?"

Sam shrugged. "He got mono. He has to do second grade again."

"You're kidding."

"Putting it in the freezer is what done it," Sam said. He turned back to the television, as though what he had said were the most reasonable thing in the world.

"You mind if I steal Vic a minute?" Mike said, and Sam looked at him with eagerness and a little fear and said, "No, sir."

They went out to the parts room. Mike handed Vic a printout of the month's re-check ratio: Royce was way ahead of the others. 38 percent of his cars were coming back. "I just had one in with a head bolt left loose," Mike said.

Vic stared at the sheet. "I'll talk to him. He's got a lot on his mind."

"Take a look at his fingernails all chewed up," Mike said. "His nose is always running. I think the guy needs to piss in a cup."

Vic pushed a hand through his hair and sighed. "You can hurt him bad with that kind of talk."

"Vic, are you blind? I got three guys to think about, not just Royce. He can't handle his recreational stuff, or he can't keep it recreational, then he's fucking up your reputation. He's fucking up *my* reputation."

The next morning Vic listened in as Royce talked to a customer, shamelessly embellishing the work he'd done. When the customer was gone, Vic came up to him. "You're not going to get a tip out of that guy."

Royce began folding up the fender mat. "Tell me about it."

"He counsels vets for a living. He's on a tight income."

Royce lit a Winston—he'd been splitting cartons with Felix—and with the filter in his lips picked up a new spark plug. "He think his work is more important than ours?"

"Than fixing cars?"

"It's no different than taking out cancer. Massaging hearts. Saving brains." He turned the spark plug but couldn't get the threads to catch in the cylinder head. He tried angle after angle. "I don't do right on a job, there's a car that cuts out on the highway. Steering locks up, he kills not only himself but the van full of church kids in the next lane over. Nearabout anyone could tip something. I mean, even waiters. Who you ever heard of had his life saved by a waiter?"

He gave up on the spark plug. Leaning against an oscilloscope, he looked at a greasy thumbnail the way you might look at a french fry. Vic saw the black under the nail and thought, Don't put that thing in your mouth.

* * *

Vic was finishing the previous day's bank deposit, a job that should've been done yesterday. But he'd spent last evening in his office trying to draft a letter to his daughter. It began with, "Honey, now that you're starting a family of your own…" and went through seven rambling pages of apologies and warnings. When he'd finished he worried that she might find some or all of it offensive and shredded the letter, hoping to approach it with a clear head at some later date in time.

He had just gotten off the phone with a bank manager, who had noticed the missed deposit, when Royce burst into his office, his hand wrapped in bloody gauze.

"How bad?" Vic said, somehow knocking his calculator off the desk as he stood. Its white receipt roll trailed across the floor.

Royce's face was flushed and gaunt, like a man who had just finished a long, strenuous run. "It's pretty hairy," he said. "A header bolt snapped. I think it about cut off a couple knuckles."

When Vic came around the desk Royce stepped back and mashed the hand to his stomach. It looked wrong. Vic glanced at the color of the stain on the bandages. He was pretty sure it was transmission fluid. "You want to go to the hospital?" he said.

Royce looked at the carpet. "I was thinking. This retired doctor fabbercated my sister a knee brace one time. He'd probably take a hundred bucks to patch me up. I go to the hospital and they jack up your liability."

"Let me see," Vic said.

"Man, I told you," Royce said, all but yelling before he caught himself. "Now I just cut the living shit out of it. You can't ever get blood out of a carpet." Royce drew the hand in again, and Vic felt a great pity that precluded any chance of playing along. When Royce glanced up Vic couldn't help but shake his head. "What are you doing, son?"

"Who says I'm doing anything?" Royce said, but it was empty, reflexive, and after a moment his face relaxed and he laughed disgustedly. "Man," he said.

"Come on, hey. It's forgotten."

Royce unwrapped the gauze and dropped it in the trash can.

"Have you talked to Maggie?"

"It's like interviewing for the toughest job in the world every time we talk." He watched Vic, his eyes shaking. "I can't calm down after. I don't want to fuck this up, Vic."

"You know, a family together is better than one apart," Vic said.

Royce closed his eyes and laced his fingers behind his head. The moment was a frail one, and as Vic struggled for meaningful words, he felt it lost. He picked his calculator up off the floor. When he turned back, Royce was rushing out the door. Vic called his name softly, not wanting to alarm the customers in the lobby, and collapsed into his chair. He stared at the desktop for nearly a minute before he realized that the deposit bag was gone.

When Vic called Sam's aunt she sounded tired and impatient and not very surprised. "He's done living here, then," she said. "I'm not housing a thief." Vic put Sam on the phone and made out enough of their exchange to understand that Sam would be sent back to relatives in New Orleans.

After work Vic drove Sam to his aunt's house. The ride was a long one over the Willamette to Springfield, and Sam stared out at the traffic. The windshield rain, shadowed by freeway lights, moved over his face in oval coins.

"Mike shouldn't have let you hear all that," Vic said. "He was just talking. I wouldn't call the police."

"Don't, okay?"

"I promise."

"Because he'll have to go to jail all over again."

Vic said nothing and felt ashamed. He switched on the radio. All week NPR had been running specials on Mardi Gras. He thought that it might help Sam feel easier, but all he could find tonight was bluegrass music. He switched it off.

"Up here is nice," Sam said. In the buttery glow of the dashboard lights it seemed impossible, but he was smiling. "I'm glad we got to come."

"Well, you fit right in," Vic said, telling himself not to offer more promises—that he would find Royce and get him clean, that Sam might come back to stay for the summer. He allowed himself to feel satisfied. They filled the rest of the ride with talk about things they had come to have in common—daytime programs, the likely engine size of the Pontiac in front of them, voodoo—until Sam pointed out the narrow street where his aunt's double-wide sat in a double-wide community, squat, square-cut azaleas and rhododendrons in front, porch lights burning, all of them trying hard to look like homes.

FROM MY WINDOW AT HOME, *by Sgt. Stuyvesant Van Veen (Wright Field, O.)*

HOW JESUS COMES

Oh God, if there's a Jesus, let him come like the class-five honeybabe that fell on us that spring day, 1976, when Coach had us sprinting 220s around the cinder track, when Aerosmith's "Walk This Way" played out the T-tops of all the jet-black Camaros as Lowman's Hardware and Grocery got hit, as did Templeton's IGA and Fred Woodhead's Feed & Seed and the slaughterhouse on the railroad track, where all the white bulls got loose and Deputy Biggs Self chased them down Main Street with the sirens blaring, fire belching out his silver-plated .45. It's all the damn truth, how a Tastee Freez straw gets driven through an oak tree and all the house trailers out at Gunter's Paradise get skinned clean as oranges. A litter of puppies gets lifted off a purebred mother and laid at the tits of a mongrel. A man gets his brains smashed out on one side of a table during a checkers game, while his twin— right across from him—suffers unspeakable serenity. The sun shines on one side of the street while apocalypse is wreaked on the other, freight trains skidding on steel rails in the midst of creepy silence. Feed-pond catfish wind the uplift vortex. Lonoke Bank

written by Michael Gills

Bank & Trust took it right on the chin—a dozen or so clerks had locked themselves up in the vault that got squeezed tight, then simply disappeared upward, delivering titles and one-hundred-year-old mortgage assessments up into the funnel's mouth. They found our stamped letters in Canada, I'm swearing to God. Nobody was about to talk that son of a bitch down, so Coach fired four blanks skyward, the last one aimed and deliberate, and goddamned the world to hell. It was the week before the Panter Relays; the pole vaulters lay down with one another in the pits, and the high jumper—Jerry Fay Hicks—cocked his red face to the sky. All the hurdlers ceased to hurdle. The big one we called Meat cast one last shot, and the discus and spear lay printed by the chalky fingerprints of the disappeared. The cross-country runners made a circle of themselves in the infield, praying and meditating the way distance men will.

And now our chins yanked up to the pink-ribbed sky, the hooked tail and twisted shoulders. *What a friend we have in Jesus! Come for us as a thief in the night!* Brother Dellwood Walker'd screamed the Sunday before at First Baptist, with its steeple jutting up over Cherry Avenue. First-team sprint relay ran a slow quarter mile, one behind the other, saying *stick* so the runner in front would raise his arm behind his back, splay fingers, take the baton, and, in turn, say *stick*, the way we'd seen Larry Gunn from Wabbaseka do it in warm-ups with the gray hood up over his Afro, about to run a forty-six flat quarter. *Stick*, he said on the curve. *Stick*, we said on the curve. *Stick*, he said on the straight. *Stick*, we said on the straight. All around Jackrabbit Stadium while the pole vaulters lay down with one another and Jerry Fay Hicks said *fuck this shit* and cleared six-eight. It came over the visitors'-side bleachers, about to rip up the stretch of green lined Bermuda where I'd made an eighty-yard run one autumn night when the frosty air was sweet with Stickum Coach had sprayed on my hands, about to destroy, even, the fifty-yard line where I'd once made love to Carrie Joe Scott, my girlfriend's big sister, one night after passing

out at Grandma Dee's hospital room and waking up with this girl's sweet-smelling breasts in my face. Please, Jesus—if you're who you say you are, come home as the tornado that shines full of fish. Shine like the golden faces of shocked cheerleaders in the drainage ditch where we took refuge. Their red-pleated skirts flew up over their heads and one screamed out in prayer, "Oh Jesus, I'll use my mouth again, please," and another cried out, "I will never ever with Bill Lingo's daddy," and another, "Oh Lord, he'll not be tasting me again," and the one boy cheerleader, goat-eyed and pink-faced, he bit back his confession. All these voices got caught up and twisted with sheets of tin shining. The sun was full out and glorious rainbows and Albino

Catfish crowed down on the green grass carpet where the upturned faces of beautiful sixteen- and seventeen-year-old girls confessed the almighty sins of this carnal world, a harmony I too joined on my knees. I prayed for Mama and O.W. and Jimmy, for Grandma Dee and for sweet Traceleen's blues and my own pitiful self. A gum wrapper slapped my face with the full force of a man's fist.

And the black tornado over us was slow and deliberate and real, the sunshine coming through its thick shoulders where all relations of matter were made one. On my knees, I stared into it, the glittering fish and tin and Lonoke County dust. I loved it with my heart's heart. She crossed Highway 89 and moved over the junior high school, over the wood desk where my brother's blond head was cradled, ten years before he'd go headfirst through the windshield into a tree trunk out on 319. Mama saw a white bull headshot by the deputy right in our front yard, the fairy blood pooling there. O.W. was hammer down through Kentucky at the time, thirty thousand pounds of slaughter turkey in tow.

And then the wind stilled and the girls' skirts righted themselves, which I was sorry to see, especially for the sake of Fonda Whitehurst, whose purple panties seemed ripeful of the storm itself, whose confession has always held for me the most heft. "Little girl, daughter," she said. "Forgive me for what I've done. I'll comfort you.

Where you are, sweetie, I'll come home to you. Your Mama loves you," she said, and I knew she meant it. And it was then, right as love rolled off Fonda's lips, that the great black tornado of 1976 chose to let us be. The sun shone clear and red-headed hummingbirds dive-bombed us from the visitors' side. A ways toward town, the twister gleamed and we got up off our hands and knees. We grinned at each other and turned red. I put an arm around Fonda Whitehurst's pale shoulders; she was my sister now. Off in the distance, the bank exploded. People died that second. *Dear God*, Fonda said with this holy white light on her face, shining through the coils of her black hair.

Sirens sang out in the eerie light. Newly bound, we stepped into the deformed world.

CASA DE GONZALES, *by Sgt. Phillip B. Hicken (Mitchell General Hospital, Cal.)*

PORCUS OMNIVORUS

You know you're dreaming because you've seen this sneaker moving like this before. The movement you're seeing is not voluntary. There's an outside force. Something else is moving the foot and with it the sneaker. A hog.

The sneaker is a Reebok, white and baby blue, reasonably clean, its laces tied neatly. It bobs up and down several times, then comes to a gradual, bouncy stop for a few moments of pregnant immobility, then goes through a few sideways moves that make one of the lace loops sway like a noose, after which there's another wicked stretch of time in which the sneaker is not moving because the hog is chewing. You can't see the hog but you know it's chewing because you've seen the sneaker move and then not move like this before. You've seen it so many times it's boring, like the back of your own hand, like your own dick. Bosnian Muslims don't eat pigs but pigs have no problem eating Bosnian Muslims. Or anybody else. They have no problem eating dead meat. It's all very boring. And before the close-up of the moving sneaker widens enough to show a whole human leg and the hog munching

written by Ismet Prcic

on its thigh, stopping to chew, then digging in again, making the lace loop sway, you come to on a sofa in someone's house in the Valley.

Yesterday, after work, your coworkers said there was a party, that you should come. You took a ride with some of them because you didn't want to drive because Jason gave you speed and pot and you felt keyed up and groggy at the same time. They promised to drive you back to your car but here you are still in the Valley on a Saturday, sweating all over someone's couch.

The sofa sags like clammy old tits. The ceiling has a cellulite problem and from a poster on the wall a white man and a black man are pointing their guns at you, about to blow you away. On the coffee table there's an array of remote controls, some smut magazines, mounds of pistachio shells, and a soldier's helmet half-full of peanut M&Ms. You swing your feet to the carpet and sit up. The air around you is yeasty with half-drunk, abandoned beers. You try to remember whose place this is but can't picture any faces. It scares you, this inability. What if they don't remember you, either? What if, after coming across you lying on their sofa, glistening, they decide to call the cops on you? You stand up, trying to make no noise.

On top of the paranoia you feel like shit. You feel like someone went through your intestinal tubing with a blowtorch. You're buzzing with this unreachable, untreatable pain. You're vibrating with it. You pick up a long-dead beer from underneath the table and pound it.

There's a short, plosive sound somewhere, a door closing or a collision of two things, then a screech of metal against metal as a shower curtain is pulled open, a gush of water against bathtub enamel. You set the bottle silently on the table and locate the front door. The next moment you're outside, running across the grass, past parked SUVs and mailboxes and driveway hoops, everywhere underneath the scorching California sun that sits smack in the middle of the merciless blue void.

The Valley is a hellhole with palm trees, a perpetual quasi-suburbia. You walk briskly for about fifteen minutes and wouldn't be able to find your way back even if you wanted to. Neighborhood-watch signs make you queasy. You think you see curtains move in the windows. There's a brawny bald fellow tinkering intrepidly inside the gaping crocodile mouth of an El Camino in his driveway, and you dash across the street to avoid him.

You need a ride. You need a ride or a way to call for a ride, probably a phone. It's a long way back to Thousand Oaks from here.

You check your pockets and find a guitar pick, some bitten-off nails, a rolled-up Save-On receipt, and no coins. Your wallet has your driver's license, an ATM card, your Bosnian ID card, some business cards with chicken scratches on the backs of them, names and numbers, idiotic ideas, makeshift maps, book titles, band names, bullshit. There's no money, which means you'll have to find an ATM, get out a twenty, take it to a store somewhere and break it up, then find a pay phone. You think if you just follow a major street you'll eventually hit a mini-mall.

Mostly there aren't any sidewalks. Walking is discouraged in the Valley. Motorists at red lights gawk at you like What is this guy doing walking, or avoid your eyes and lock their doors.

You've seen pigs eat dead villagers: big, pink, fleshy hogs feeding on gray, wet, dead people. You've seen other things, too—chopped-off heads near makeshift goalposts, human-ear necklaces, dickless, toothless, breastless, scrotumless, noseless, eyeless, fingerless, armless, headless, legless, pissed on, shat on, come on, carved up, stabbed through, burned, bludgeoned, fucked-with bodies of men and women you knew. You've seen all this and yet the images that come back to you now, night after night, nap after nap, are from the TV footage you saw toward the beginning of war: a close-up of a sneaker, moving then stopping then moving again until a slow pan reveals the hog.

Memory is bullshit.

Stop it.

You make yourself look around. Corner of Somewhere and Someplace. The crosswalk signal is red. Cars are zooming by: an Asian lady in white, a fat redhead smoking a cigarette, a man with a thin moustache, a hippie stereotype in a tie-dyed VW van, a police cruiser. You can't stand standing there.

There's a song in your head, something accordiony from back home. You think about firing bullets into unsuspecting bodies, rib cages ripping open, heads caving, oozing stuff. The music in your head gets louder and you realize that it's not exclusively in your head.

A man wearing black slacks and a wifebeater stumbles out of a beige house and opens a tall door to the backyard, where apparently someone is playing a song you know on an accordion. He's yelling into his cell phone and it takes a surreal mo-ment for you to realize that he's speaking Bosnian.

"...park it on the grass, then, I guess— fuck it!" he says, then waves to someone behind you.

You turn around and find a burgundy minivan there, its driver with one hand on the wheel and the other holding a cell phone to his ear, waiting for you to get out of the way. As soon as you hop aside he has the minivan slanted up the gentle slope of the lawn, its fender kissing a rosebush. You look up and down the street. There isn't a parking spot in sight for miles. It's another party. With Bosnians this time.

Out of the van comes a gaggle of boys and girls, all of them screeching in English. The wifebeater man makes them all high-five him before he lets them squeeze by and fuck off into the backyard.

"*Domacine*," says the driver, locking the van with one of those key remotes. *Be-beep!* Both men raise their arms like they haven't seen each other for years, step into a hearty hug, then smack kisses on each other's cheeks, three apiece.

"Come on in, come in!"

"Did you start without me?"

"Shit yeah, we started last night."

"I heard, I heard!"

The driver walks toward the door, then realizes that the man in the wifebeater hasn't moved.

"Are you coming?"

"Yeah, I just want to smoke a cigarette in peace. Go get yourself a beer."

"Hurry up."

You watch all this like it's a play; it isn't until the man in the wifebeater gives you a look that you realize you're just standing there, staring at him lighting up. He's thick and meaty, older than you, with thinning black hair held up and against his skull with what must be bucketfuls of gel, all of it painstakingly combed to give the whole head a ribbed texture, like in mafia pictures.

"You want one?" he says to you in English.

You don't usually like talking to Bosnians in America. You feel like they stand in the way of your complete assimilation. You don't like the doubling of words in your head, things coming out in Bonglish.

But then you remember you still need to make a phone call.

"All right, give me one," you say to the man in Bosnian, watching his eyes pop open, bloodshot and blue, almost teary.

"Are you here for the thing?" he asks, lighting your cigarette, a menthol, nodding back toward the house. You get a whiff of his breath and for a second you're back with your dad and his slivovitz-drinking friends, yelling at the soccer game on TV, clapping yourself on the forehead when they just miss it by an inch, watching them swear and say stuff like "My aunt Devleta would put that in" or "Fuck his mother, he's got two left legs."

"No, man—I was just walking by and heard the music."

"Where are you from?"

"Tuzla. You?"

"The whole of Tuzla, a single goat did milk, and then keeps on bragging that it feeds on cheese." It's an old song about your town, and he's smiling like he's proud he remembers it after all these years. "I've been there a million times. My ex-girlfriend studied there. Jasna Hodzic. You knew her?"

"I don't think."

"Kind of shortish, blonde hair?"

"I don't think so."

"Tits up to here?"

"I don't think so, man."

"Man, she fucked like a pike."

He takes a drag, a sad toke of nicotine fumes and nostalgia, looking glassily away. You try to emulate him.

"She got blown up by our own shell," he says, and smokes. You don't know what to tell him, so you just ape his mannerisms. You read in *How to Make Friends* that it puts strangers at ease.

"I told her a million times to fuckin' get out," he continues, but then stops himself. Something like anger blows across his face. His eyes change. "Oh, fuck her. *Her* fuckin' choice." He smokes some more and then says, in English, "There's plenty of pussy in the sea," and laughs, smacking you on the back so hard it uproots you. His cigarette is almost to the filter now, and you still have to ask about the phone.

"Listen—" you start.

"When did you get here? To the States."

"Uh... end of '95."

"How'd you get out?"

"Got wounded in battle. They let me go."

"Wait a minute, you were a soldier?"

He's suddenly very close to you, looking into your eyes like a lover or a nemesis. You nod, leaning backward. You swear to God he starts to cry a little, embraces you like he did the driver earlier and kisses you on both cheeks.

"You have to come in and party," he manages through his genuinely shrinking throat, then hugs you some more. Clamping your neck, he maneuvers you toward his house. "I won't take no for an answer. Not even in theory."

"I should—"

"My pops would love to meet you," he says, ushering you past a line of color-coded garbage bins. "He still can't forgive himself for not going back to fight when you guys needed it the most."

Most of the backyard, you see, is taken over by a long, white tent. Underneath it forty or fifty people are packed around a long table, fanning themselves with paper plates, gulping down beers, yelling, laughing, standing up to make announcements. Little kids run in and out of the house with sticks in their hands, marshmallows stuck on their tips. Their mothers run after them, screaming for them not to run. They scream in Bosnian and the kids answer in whiny English, complaining that so-and-so's mother is letting so-and-so do

what he likes, *look*. In the yard's far corner there's a kidney-shaped hole in the grass, the beginnings of a pool in which a hairy man with a T-shirt tied around his head is using the shallow end to spit-roast a pig. Something is a little off.

"Here," says the wifebeater man, handing you a Beck's. "Let's find you a spot at the table."

As you follow him you figure it out. Next to the tent there's a three-colored flag with a yellow symbol in the middle, an orthodox Christian cross and a Cyrillic S in each of its quadrants, four S's you've seen before. They stand for *Samo sloga Srbina spasava*, your enemy's creed from the war you fought in and survived. Only Unity Saves a Serb.

You look for the easiest way to get the fuck out of there. Through the house, maybe? Or across the pool, onto that bench and over the wall into someone else's yard? Definitely not the way you came. Too many bodies to go through. You're mad at yourself. You should have realized something earlier: three kisses for the Holy Trinity, not to mention the pig in the pool. Shit. You sidestep timidly toward the house.

The wifebeater man has made it to the head of the table now, and he leans in and speaks directly to someone sitting there whose face you cannot see because there's an enormous blond hairdo in your line of vision, like a clown's Afro. You don't see him until he stands up, wobbly on his feet, this perfervid patriarch dressed in Chetnik war paraphernalia, *sajkaca*, *kokarda*, greasy gray beard down to his bellybutton, a pistol grip protruding from his pants.

"Where is this soldier man?" he yells, looking around while his son tries to keep him standing. He speaks in a patchy Serbian dialect with a rural Bosnian lilt, only a Bosnian Serb, a wannabe. You're six feet from the back door when his hammered eyes finally find your own. The man smiles and waves you over.

Running right now would not be a good thing. A calm voice from within tells you to do what you're told. You raise your bottle to the man and take a royal swig to buy yourself some time, then saunter over. Some of the people around the table pat your back. Those that can't reach you raise their glasses in your honor, then go back to their conversations.

"Make some room for the war hero," snarls the patriarch at the clown-fro lady, who has a face full of deviled egg.

"I'm done anyway," she blurts, spraying egg bits out of her mouth as she stands. The wifebeater man and his pops shepherd you into her seat. Up close you can see that the old man has an elaborate tattoo on his shriveling forearm, a black shield with a red and blue border. In its center floats a two-headed eagle with two yellow swords held crossed beneath a human skull. Cyrillic letters are inked above and below it. *FOR KING AND FATHER-LAND. FREEDOM OR DEATH.*

In 1993, your unit crawled through a sticky minefield to take out a machine-gun nest as prep work for the early-morning offensive. The Claw, the leader of the unit and a truly insane individual, crept into the nest without his boots on and stabbed the last Chetnik in the back. He came out with a souvenir, a banner with an identical skull-and-swords design. A pirate flag, he called it.

The patriarch claps your back and squeezes your arm, telling you how his dad was a Chetnik in the Second World War under the direct command of General Draza Mihajlovic and so were both of his brothers, and how he, the youngest, was too young to fight back then and how his father liked him the least because of that, sent him to *Chemerica* without a dinar to carve a place for himself in the world. As he talks you start thinking of a different way to get out of here. Plum brandy.

"We should have a toast for staying alive despite everything," you say, and swig your beer again.

"Wait for us," the son says, looking around for his beverage.

"You're gonna toast with beer?" You turn to the old man. "We need something stronger for this, right?"

"He's right," the father says. "Milosh, go get the *rakija*."

An effete, shuddering fan trained on the back of the old man's head putters to a stop. He swears, leans down to the grass, and fumbles with its cord until, resuscitated, it starts to twirl again, halfheartedly.

"Connection," the old man explains.

You clink your beer against his and you both drink. He starts to talk again.

"See, both of my brothers were savagely killed. Dragisha, God save his soul, was caught and executed by the partisans in 1942 or 1943, we are not sure exactly when. His body was never found. Zdravko, God save his soul, was axed to death by the *Zeleni Kadar* in northeastern Bosnia. Fucking Turks. They chopped him up into pieces like a birch log. He came back to us in four burlap sacks."

He slams his fist on the table like he's in a bad play. Deviled eggs jiggle on his plate. His eyes well up. You hold his gaze while tightening your lips and shake your head in your best approximation of commiseration.

"After that my father hated me, said that if I'd been with my brothers to watch their backs they wouldn't be dead now. But I was only twelve years old."

Milosh comes back with a plastic Fanta bottle full of yellowy liquid and a tray of clashing, mismatched shot glasses. As he passes by her a woman in black stands up from the table.

"What do you want that for?" she booms at him. She has a mouthful of gleaming golden teeth.

"To drink."

"You want to kill your father?"

"He told me to get it for a toast."

"It's the middle of the day and he's drunk already. You'll give him a heart attack in this heat."

"*Rakija* thins the blood, Mother," he says, and puts a shot glass in front of his father and another in front of you. He fills them all the way to the lip and then pours himself one as well.

"To survival despite the enemy's best efforts at achieving otherwise," you say, and raise your glass. Milosh and his father follow.

"Whiny Turkish cunts!"

"Fuck their mothers on their shitty prayer rugs!"

You hold yours up until everyone at the table who wants to join in has a beverage in their hand, then slam it to the back of your throat, feeling like someone napalmed your stomach ulcer. It takes a conscious effort to suppress your urge to vomit. It's not the brandy so much as what you're toasting to.

Your mother's body flashes in your mind's eye, a skeletal figure too brittle and head-shy to hug after her stint at the camp. You shake your head to get it off your mind. In her stead emerge fallen trench-mates, their faces rigid and pale like papier-mâché masks. And before the floodgates are open all the way you slap yourself, hard.

More toasts are shouted from all around the table: toasts to dead relatives, to dead relatives' saints, to the personal saints of the host's family members (his name is Jovan Cvetkovic, you hear), to slogans like Serbia-to-Tokyo, to President Milosevic, etc. Every time a shot goes down Jovan's gullet he tries to stand up, pull out his weapon, and fire into the air, but Milosh and some younger cousins step in and dissuade him. They remind him that he's in the Valley, in America. In response Jovan drops back into his chair and moans. You're livid, but the sight of that *Zastava* sticking out of the old man's pants keeps you from doing anything stupid.

Meanwhile the food's been served, and now everyone's plowing through it: soups, stuffed squash, stuffed peppers, savory pastry coils. There's an accordion player, a fat person in a green felt hat with a crow's feather stuck in the band and a moustache of a sort that vandals draw on posters. He plays and sings with various degrees of success. Every once in a while he gets a clutch of people to get up and dance *kolo*. They wave you over every time, and eventually you tell them the shrapnel in your leg cuts off your circulation when you sit for too long and Jovan yells at them not to bother you. Really there's no shrapnel, just nausea and cloying memories, confusion.

At some point they unload the pig, head and all, placing it on the table so it faces you with one eye closed and the other agape and forlorn. They pull the spit out of its ass and put half a lemon in its mouth. They pour beer over it and laugh and smack their lips and ask for cutlery. They're all really happy.

You're ripping apart. You see your mother climbing through an open window in Tuzla and your arms grab for her in the Valley. Your muscles remember how they had to hold on to her when she bucked and shrieked that day, trying to end it. Let me go, you hear her say, and the people around you dig into the pig. Your arms are rigid, holding on to nothing. Your stomach climbs into your chest. The sneaker moves in your mind, then doesn't. You want to run away or cry or start swinging.

In your heart you don't know what you want. When some woman serves you a big, glistening piece of flesh you throw up all over it, all over the plate, the side of the table, your lap. Somebody tilts your chair and you hit the grass, still vomiting.

"Lightweight," you hear Milosh say. You kneel there.

The woman, the clown-head, helps you up. She walks you through the back door and into the house, shielding your head with her hand when you pass below a chandelier, and puts you in front of the bathroom door. She knocks.

"Hold your horses," says a female voice from inside.

She raises your head.

"Are you all right?"

You grunt.

"Are you sure?"

You nod.

"Okay. Wait until she's done and use the bathroom."

"Thank you," you manage, covering your mouth for her benefit.

"Don't puke on my carpet now," she says, smiling. Then she's gone.

You look around the hallway. Pictures everywhere, collages: Jovan in a Chetnik uniform, Jovan in a suit, younger Jovan with the '70s lamb chops and moustache, his wife in a floral-patterned dress, hugging a baby to her chest. A family portrait with a head-count of more than a hundred. Milosh as a child on a donkey at the beach somewhere, Milosh on prom night with a blonde date, Milosh at the wheel of a red Camaro. A huge portrait of General Draza Mihajlovic with his round little glasses and the puff around his eyes and a beard to match Jovan's, only blacker. Next to it, framed in thin wood, is a photograph of a purplish medal. You get closer to read the caption and are stunned. It says:

General Dragoljub Mihajlovic distinguished himself in an outstanding manner as Commander-in-Chief of the Yugoslavian Armed Forces and later as Minister of War by organizing and leading important resistance forces against the enemy which occupied Yugoslavia from December 1941 to December 1944. Through the undaunted efforts of his troops, many United States airmen were rescued and returned safely to friendly control. General Mihajlovic and his forces, although lacking adequate supplies, and fighting under extreme hardships, contributed materially to the Allied cause and were materially instrumental in obtaining a final Allied Victory.

—Legion of Merit award citation given by Harry S. Truman, President, The White House, March 29, 1948

Underneath, in Cyrillic longhand, someone has written:

The highest award the U.S. government can bestow upon a foreign national.

You don't know what to think. Your whole life, since you were six years old, your teachers have told you that Draza Mihajlovic was a bad man, a quisling, someone who fought with the Nazis against the Yugoslav army and ordered the slaughter of a lot of Yugoslavians who were not of his faith. But here he is, an ordained American hero. You stagger away in rage. In fear.

No one's come out of the bathroom yet. You go farther down the corridor, into a bedroom, and find a phone. You dial your apartment and after two rings your roommate picks up.

"Hello."

"Eric, I need a ride from you, dude. I'm in a pickle."

"Where are you?"

"In the Valley."

"Still at that party?"

"No, I'm in the house of a psycho and need to get the fuck outta here, pronto."

"Can it wait? I'm making ramen."

"You should be in the car right now, dude."

As you say "dude" there are four pistol shots in rapid succession: *BANG-BANGBANGBANG!* You look around and notice an envelope on the bed stand addressed to some other Cvetkovic. The mother.

"Are those gunshots?"

Ignoring the question, you read the address into the phone twice. You're pleading now. "Come get me, man."

You hear some commotion out in the corridor, and turn around in time to catch a glimpse of Milosh and his mother hurrying down the hall, arguing about where to hide the pistol, fussing.

You remember a cataclysmic night on the front line, when the snow was the color of bone in the close-to-full-moonlight and the branches were spread above you like blood vessels on the anemic belly of the night sky and the bullets dove from nowhere, crashing into soft things and bouncing off hard things, and the enemy mortars smashed everything into powder. You remember the story The Claw told you that night, the one about how, some time ago, he was given orders to crawl up a hill and rendezvous with another squad of guys who were crawling up from the other side. He was supposed to wear a white band around his left arm to distinguish himself from the enemy, since otherwise their uniforms were virtually identical. He told you about how he reached the top and lizarded his way into a trench full of guys with white armbands on their left arms, squatting there, shooting the shit, until finally he realized that they were actually Chetniks, that by some strange twist of fate they'd decided on the same white armband to set themselves apart. You see The Claw keeping his cool, creeping backward, silently cocking his Kalashnikov and killing them all from behind.

The bathroom's open now and you lock yourself in, determined to wait it out. The little room is decorated in belabored beige: beige tiles, beige shower curtain, red and beige towels, your own beige face in the mirror. You splash water on yourself, take some into your mouth, spit it out, take it in and spit it out. Through the small, pebbled window you can see the accordion player typing an intricate Balkanesque melody onto two keyboards simultaneously, acting like no shots were fired at all. You sit on the beige toilet lid, put your head into your beige hands and stare at the tile grid on the floor, at a wastebasket, at the grid again. You think of death and mother. You try to figure out what's right.

The wastebasket is small, wicker, and lined with plastic. You push at the base of it with the edge of your foot and the wads of tissue tumble and rearrange themselves, exposing a dull glint beneath. You reach in and retrieve Jovan's gun.

Your hand knows what to do with it; your index finger turns inward. The grip feels good. You sniff the barrel and it smells of youth, of Bosnia. You switch the safety off and stand up. You cock. In the mirror you look like The Claw, standing there against the beige. You lean closer. Your eyes are all pain.

Police sirens start off low and grow higher until they shut up the accordion player and silence the clamoring Serbs. There are conversations you can't really hear. Questions are asked. Things are blamed on the kids, fireworks. Apologies are given and warnings issued. You realize you're standing there with a gun in your hand. Where is Eric? How long does it take to get here from Thousand Oaks in an Oldsmobile?

You pace the bathroom. You hide the gun. You pick it up again. Hide it. Pick it up. You lift the tank lid, toss the gun in. You close the tank.

Half an hour later a car horn sounds and you know it's your ride. There's a party going on in the backyard again. You focus on what you need to do, take a deep breath, and get out of the bathroom and down the corridor. There are kids sitting around the table in the kitchen, laughing. You make your way across the living room. The white front door is the only thing you see. You can feel it, this elation in your chest, this glee in the muscles of your face. Your lips curl. You reach for the doorknob and wrap your fist around it.

"Soldier!" Jovan yells from behind you. "Where are you going?"

He stumbles toward you, pushing himself off the walls, almost falls but doesn't. He makes it to the back of the giant armchair and, with fifteen or so feet without anything to balance himself on ahead of him, stops there and leans on it with both hands.

"Stay awhile longer."

"I have to go, sir. I didn't mean to stay this long. I have some things I have to do."

He grunts. "Eh, okay. Okay, but come over here before you go so I can thank you for what you've done for us."

He raises his arms, stumbles forward, and catches himself just before he hits the back of the chair with his face. The car horn sounds again. You can see the brown Delta 88 right in front of the house.

"That's my ride," you tell him, and start to step out the door.

"Tell me one thing."

You wait. You turn to him.

"How many of them did you—" he stops, dragging his left forefinger across his neck, "—with your own hand?"

You look at him, this son of a bitch. His eyes smirk. You want to say *I'm Mustafa Nalic* but you can't. You want to forgive him. In your heart you want to hug him but you're afraid you'd break his spine. You want to shake his hand but you're afraid you'd pull his whole arm out of its socket. You want to kiss his cheek and spit upon it.

You don't know what you want.

"One night I infiltrated an enemy trench and killed six with one clip. They thought I was one of them. They were joking around. I just mowed them all down."

He smiles and nods his head.

"Good for you," he says.

FORT PUTNAM, WEST POINT, *by Glen A. Heberling (U.S. Military Academy)*

PENTIMENTO

PART TWO

"My father passed when I was fourteen," Jen says, holding Nkiru's hand. Nkiru grunts something like condolences and squeezes Jen's hand tighter. "My mother picked me up from school that afternoon and took me to get ice cream. I thought maybe she'd gotten my report card or something. Then we went to Rock Creek Park, just behind the zoo. It was summertime and there were mothers and their young kids running around." Jen looks up to the lights. "She said it's just you, me, and your brothers now, baby. And then she held me while I cried."

"How did he die?" Nkiru asks.

"Cancer. He was sick for a while."

"Can we get coffee?" Nkiru asks a moment later, as they shiver down the street toward her car. The black Mercedes still has its hazard lights on. There's a pink ticket slipped under the wiper, the sight of which is strangely comforting. The world does go on, it says. Jen takes the keys from Nkiru's hand and slides them into the door.

They stop at a coffee shop near Dupont Circle. Jen attempts to park, starting forward, lurching backward, adjusting and

written by Uzodinma Iweala

readjusting until the taxi drivers begin cursing in a mixture of English and Amharic. Nkiru doesn't notice. "Come on," Jen urges. Inside, Jen orders two coffees, black without sugar, and sets them on the table. Nkiru breathes in the steam, coughs, and breathes deeply again.

"My son," she says. "This will kill him." Her tears drop onto the tabletop, into the coffee, and onto her fingers, running down to the webs between. Jen offers napkins and a warm hand, the left one, diamond ring and gold band glinting beneath the café's track lighting. Nkiru begins to cry harder.

"How old is Victor again? Twenties?" Jen asks, trying to stem Nkiru's tears. "He's a strong man. Don't underestimate him."

"You don't understand—they were just getting to know each other. Just now, now that Victor is at college, now that he and his father couldn't be stubborn in the same way, in the same place." All the noise, all the shouting, the open hostility had all but vanished, replaced by something like mutual respect, almost an open friendship. Lately she'd caught them laughing, Christopher's hand on his son's curly head of hair. Or the two of them—son slightly taller and darker—standing outside on the front porch at night, shushing her as they watched a doe and her fawn trekking across the lawns and eating the neighbors' tulips.

*　*　*

UZODINMA IWEALA

Christopher wasn't there when Victor was born. Nobody was—not her father, mother, or sister, although Nkiru had written to them each month as her stomach grew rounder. She and Christopher went to Lamaze classes together, bought baby toys together, and made love on their sides, slowly and carefully, his fingers stretched wide over the bump of her belly. Then one night he told her that he would have to travel, for two weeks only.

"I'll be back before the baby comes."

"What?" she whispered, holding his arm around her body as they lay atop sweat-dampened sheets. "Christopher, no! You promised."

"I know," he said, and then hesitated, because he knew how she reacted to the word *but*. In these later stages of her pregnancy she had become bored and irritable. She complained constantly that the apartment was too small, or too noisy. She felt that the people on the street were watching her. "They are, too," she would say.

"You aren't serious," she said then, gripping Christopher's arm tightly. "So I'm supposed to walk into the hospital alone? No husband. No mother. No father?" He winced.

"Love," he said. "I have to go. The USSR is opening up. There are deals—career-making deals."

"Where are you going?" she asked.

"Kazakhstan—natural gas. Lots of it."

"And when your son comes into this

world without a father to hold him? What will you say it was that kept you? Natural gas?"

"What about a father without a job?"

Nkiru sat up on the edge of the mattress and crossed her ankles over the edge.

"I will be back well before you're due, love." Christopher sat up behind her and played with her braids. "Two weeks. Only two weeks. We'll be all the better for it. I promise."

"No girls?" she asked. Christopher winced again. Nkiru asked that question each time he left on business; for the most part, he'd learned to ignore it. And each trip abroad, at the bar, assaulted by long legs, short skirts, and low-cut tops, he would remember that night on the bank of the Thames when Nkiru tossed her wedding ring into the black waters.

"In two weeks I'll be holding you in one arm and our baby girl in the other."

"Boy," Nkiru said.

"Girl."

"Boy," she said, and pushed him down. They lay there laughing until the sweat began all over again.

Christopher didn't come back in time. Victor came early, three weeks early, forcing his mother to the hospital from the supermarket down the street from their apartment. Nkiru arrived alone, like one of the younger black women hospital staff detested so much. Husbandless and unable to say much over the pain, she could only huff to the nurses Call my doctor, please call this doctor. They looked at her, half shaking their heads even while she panted medical terms to prove who she was. "Am I dilated enough? CHINEKE IT HURTS! What is my heart rate? JESUS CHRIST LORD IN HEAVEN GHENTI OH!" Some hours later, after the urine-stained sheets were removed, her baby lay in her arms, almost white with such a small face and a little button nose. A boy. She had forced the name Victor on Christopher—a compromise. It wasn't Igbo as she'd wanted, but it was her father's Christian middle name.

* * *

In truth, Jen does not understand. She had, because of her father's long illness, never really known the man. Where her friends' fathers stood upright and able to lift them high above their heads, hers had always been weak and distant. In truth, Jen cried at the park to make her mother feel better. Of course she'd felt sadness, but not the stinging, squeezing pain that losing the child between her first and last had brought and left to linger. "Victor will be a man," she hears herself say.

There is a sudden resolve in Nkiru that comes out as a fist on the table. Their coffee shakes but doesn't slosh from the cups. "I can go to Boston," she mumbles, and shivers at the thought of that New England cold—her son had said once, "The saliva freezes on my teeth, Mom!" Christopher had started laughing, singing "Give me the tropics any day. The bite of Benin takes my breath away!"

"I can go there. Yes. Yes I can. Tell him. Hold him. Let him cry on me. Yes. And then, after the funeral, we'll go somewhere. How can I buy tickets? Where can I buy tickets?" Then she slumps again. "But who will take care of everything here? Shit! This is where an uncle or aunt would have been lovely. I mean nothing about this is lovely, but you know what I mean," she pleads, holding her palms out toward Jen, tracing their deep brown lines with her eyes. They become fists again as she thinks of her family. "How could they?" she whispers.

* * *

"How could they not write back?" she asked, when he told her to stop checking the mail every five minutes. "A child, their grandchild, was born. Their first one." Victor slept, for once barely audible, a blessing for both of them because he cried so much. Christopher had invested in earplugs—bright bits of orange foam that looked like carrots growing from his ears. Nkiru teased him constantly. But tonight the boy slept deeply, his hands reaching up at intervals and his small fingers playing in the light.

"Christopher, look at him. Can you believe they don't want to know about him?"

"Come, love," Christopher said, drawing her away from the crib and out into the living room. "I can't imagine a man as smart as your father being so stupid for so long."

"He's not stupid. Just very traditional."

"Why do you defend him, Nkiru? You can only do your best. Let God do the rest."

"That sounds mighty Nigerian of you," she said.

They hired someone, Cristina, a young Filipina with dark hair and a repaired cleft palate, to take care of Victor. She came mornings at six, so Nkiru could go back to work.

"Mrs. Watsman, you need more help," the girl said one evening. "Someone who can cook and clean too—full-time."

Nkiru didn't do much but nod and reach for her purse for the day's pay. But when Christopher came home that night a bit later than usual, livelier than usual, smelling of alcohol and cigarettes, she brought it up. He pulled her up from the couch and danced her around the room—bumping them both into the coffee table, the television. "You're right. You're right," he sang. "But to do that we need a house and to buy a house we need money for a down payment. And quarter bonuses just came in."

"Oh, Christopher!" Nkiru hugged him close and kissed him deeply.

"Let's go out," he said.

"The baby."

"Let's order in, then."

"Okay," she said. "Chinese, Thai?" Nkiru stepped into the kitchen and began to open drawers, searching for the take-out menus. The day's mail was on the kitchen counter—a stack of bills, an airmail envelope, thin and white. She stared at it. "My sister," she said.

Christopher had gone to check on Victor. Nkiru followed him with a table knife between the folds of the envelope. *Years ago, you left us, me, without saying goodbye. Mummy and Daddy are fine—same as ever—they argue, then kiss. Mummy still goes to church, me a bit less so... Congratulations on your new baby Victor—I wish I could see him—pass my well wishes to the new father!... I was recently married—*

Victor was awake, crying. Christopher lifted him up, but the boy stretched out his arms for his mother. "Oh, for God's sake," Christopher said. "It's me. Daddy. Vic. Victor." But the boy would have none of it. Nkiru took him. Victor began to play with her face.

"My God," she said. She held the letter out to Christopher. "My sister. She's married. I've missed so much."

"They've missed so much," Christopher said. "Why didn't your sister—" He scanned the pages. "She says your father forbade her to invite you."

"So she thought it better just not to tell me? Not to tell me!" Nkiru sat down on the bed, setting the baby beside her. "Mommy loves you," she said.

"And Daddy loves you too," added Christopher.

"Does he need to know now?" Jen asks.

Nkiru's eyes answer, Are you stupid?

"I mean—what I mean is, you don't have to go to Boston now, Nkiru. You need strength and composure. You need to be strong for him." Jen is talking faster than her tongue can manage. Nkiru looks around.

"Let's leave," she says. "We'll go to the cathedral, do you mind?"

There are schoolboys without winter coats blowing vapor into the air as they cross the greens in front of the massive church, toward the bronze doors. "Forty-five years in this city," Jen says, "and I've never been inside."

"Never? You're not religious?"

"I'm Jewish."

"Hmm. I didn't know that," Nkiru says, bowing her head. Her mother would hate this church—so empty that echoes chase each other around the pillars, so formal with its rigid wooden pews. "When I was younger, we brought our own bibles," Nkiru says, picking up a prayer book. "I never really liked it. My father made me go until I told him he should come too, if I had to." She pauses for a moment. "I said it in front of his friends and he didn't like it. He gave me a beating that evening. But I didn't have to go again."

"Well done," says Jen.

"Christopher is an atheist—was an atheist," Nkiru corrects herself. "So is Victor. He could have been the son my father never had. If only—well."

Her sister said as much when she visited them in Washington, after they'd moved into the house on Morrison Street, where the neighbors had asked her if she was the new housekeeper, where Victor, as he ate Cheerios off the kitchen counter, asked her one weekend, "Why does Daddy talk with a funny voice? And why aren't you white?"

Nkiru told Chinwe what her son had said while they sat with Christopher at the dinner table, cups of tea in front of them. Her sister—always considered the prettier of the two, now grown thick around her stomach and neck, with the flabby, Christian-mother arms they used to laugh about, the ones that flapped when devout women raised their hands in praise at church.

"Well, you can't make America less racist," Chinwe responded. "Less confusing for a child like Victor. Especially Victor."

"What do you mean?" Christopher asked, drumming his fingers against the table. Nkiru put a hand on his leg, but he brushed it aside. "My son knows perfectly well who and what he is."

"All I'm saying is that Nigeria is a much simpler place to raise a child," Chinwe said. "Away from the confusion. Surrounded by family."

"Oh, you all know quite a lot about

family," Christopher blurted out. He took a slurp of too-hot tea from his mug and squeezed his face.

"We're not perfect," Chinwe ventured cautiously. She looked directly at Nkiru. "None of us are."

"What does he want me to do?" Nkiru asked later, after Christopher excused himself and crept upstairs to bed. "Divorce my husband?"

"Just say you're sorry. That's it." How many times had they been like this? When Nkiru talked back to their parents, Chinwe smoothed it over. She put syrup on the words.

"Apologize for loving my husband and my son?" Nkiru stood up. "The son they haven't even bothered to meet?"

"Ki Ki, please!" Nkiru hadn't heard that name in a decade. She sat down, scraping her chair against the floor. "You would not be apologizing for them."

"Then for what? My life? Have I done badly since leaving? Have I failed? I'm a surgeon, a mother, a wife."

"You used to be someone's daughter."

"Is that my fault? Look, Chinwe—I'm happy. Why can't they be happy for me?"

"Are you happy? You have no family here. What will you do when you grow old? Who will take care of you? Don't you think you want to be at home?"

"I left home because my family abandoned me."

"Or did you abandon us?"

"Oh, come on. I abandoned ignorance."

"For what? Isolation? There is a reason why old men say a foolish man is a happy man."

"Save your proverbs, Chinwe. This isn't Nigeria."

"If he doesn't want a service, what does he want?"

"I don't know," Nkiru says. "I suppose… well, I don't know. We used to live there," she says, pointing up to a redbrick apartment block with white stripes marking each story. "Right in the shadow of God." Her old apartment window holds a row of plants thick and green across the sill. We never had plants, she thinks. "Someone will have to tell Christopher's office," she says. "Someone will have to write an obituary."

"Yes," Jen says. "But in good time."

Back in the car, they cruise past naked shrubbery and salt-stained driveways as they cut across town toward her house. Elementary-school children in puffy, bright-colored coats and cartoon-character backpacks skip behind their condensed breath. "Doesn't someone need to get your son from school?" Nkiru asks. "You don't need to stay with me. You've done too much already."

"Nanny" is all Jen says, giving a quick glance to the trembling woman next to her. A minute later they pull into Nkiru's driveway.

"Chineke! I left the front door wide open. Imagine that. My husband is dead so rob me." Nkiru forces a laugh that sounds more like a stray dog's yelp. Her braids whisper as she shakes her head.

With Jen just behind, she stands at the threshold of the front door, her head stuck into the interior darkness, her fingers flat against the faded red brick. "Is anybody home? Anybody at all?" she calls out. Jen can't help but cover her mouth to hold back a sob. A quick jacket sleeve to her eyes. "Go on," she says, nudging Nkiru slightly. They creep in, stopping to watch the white curtains billow over the living room couch. Picture frames shine brass and silver. They move through the dining room into the brightly lit kitchen,

all stainless steel and black granite, and then Nkiru stops before the back stairs. Next to them the door to Christopher's study is open. His chair, the brown leather executive that he "borrowed" from his office, faces the hall. "He sat here when he said it," she says.

"Said what?" Jen asks.

She shivers. This cold. This silence. This emptiness is too much.

"We should do wills, love," Christopher said one night, when Nkiru came home a bit earlier than usual.

"What's gotten into you?" she asked, taking a moment to remove her flats and jacket. "No 'hi' for me? No kiss and 'how was your day?'"

Christopher watched his wife let down her braids from her ponytail. "Where's Victor?" she asked, glancing up the stairs to the door of her son's bedroom.

"Friday night, love. Leslie's house."

"When is he back?"

"He called to say that he'd be spending the night there, in her bed. Her parents are okay with it so I said why not." Nkiru wedged her eyebrows together. "Come now," Christopher said. "He'll be home by twelve."

"You know I don't like him there that late. It's not proper."

"Like someone didn't want you somewhere at some point in your life."

She frowned, and started up the stairs.

"Nkiru, wait—seriously, though. We need to do wills. What if?"

"What if you quit smoking again and followed your doctor's orders?"

"You're not my doctor, darling."

"Oh, for God's sake, Christopher, leave me alone. I'm not in the mood."

"One of the other partners—his son died."

"What! You don't mean it. Which one?"

"Betford."

"Jesus Christ of Nazareth. God forbid bad thing," she said, sitting down on the steps. Christopher stood there looking up at her, his hands hanging helplessly by his sides.

"Twenty-four years old. Just out of university. He was a marine."

"Terrible," Nkiru said, shaking her head. She remembered that man and his coldness, the wife's slightly southern accent and her unwillingness to acknowledge that Nkiru was a surgeon. "But what does that have to do with you?" she asked Christopher now. "You're not a soldier."

"But we do have projects there, and I am a managing partner. And that means—"

"I forbid you to go. You can't go."

"I never said I was going. But London might ask someone for—"

"London can go and screw itself. You are not going. Period. What would Victor and I do?"

"All the same, we aren't young anymore and anything can happen. You never know what or when, Nkiru."

"Christopher. STOP IT!" she said. She stormed up the stairs. He heard the bedroom door slam a moment later. That night, next to each other, waiting for the *beep beep* of the alarm system to tell them that Victor was home, Christopher said, "I'll quit smoking. Again. Really. And I'll start to exercise."

She placed a hand on his stomach beneath the sheets. "Skinny doesn't mean healthy, you know."

"But it does mean sexy," he said, nuzzling into her neck.

They made an appointment with a lawyer, the same one who'd handled the neighbor's lawsuit against them over the positioning of the shrubbery. Those neighbors had long since disappeared, packing themselves into a large green Mayflower moving van and their two station wagons, but the lawyer had stayed. He sent holiday cards stocked with legal humor: *What did Santa give the lawyer for Christmas? A new suit. Season's Greetings from Elliot Loestine, Esq.* He was a short man, with glasses and thinning hair he dyed brown. He had pictures of his college-age son and married daughter on his desk. "Her husband's German. Go figure," he said. They declared their assets to him, the houses—Morrison Street, the beach, and his deceased mother's Kilburn flat—the stock portfolios, the insurance plans.

"It's amazing what the years accumulate," Nkiru said. It all went to Victor, most of it in trust. Christopher was initialing in wide loops on each page when she grabbed his wrist. "No. Wait," she said. "I left out my parents. My sister."

"You left them out? Love?" Christopher asked, giving Loestine an exasperated glance.

"I know. I know. But? But there are so many other things. Where will we be buried?"

"Ah, London? I thought you said near my mother? I could have sworn you said that."

Loestine rapped the pressboard of his desk, his smile showing a green bit of lettuce on a front tooth. "Looks like you need more time. Another meeting, perhaps?"

"You always do this," Christopher said in the car home. "Big-decision time and you change your mind."

"I always do this?"

"Yes, you do. You have a hard time committing to anything."

"Ah ah! See me trouble. Commitment? Where was she from again? Oh yes. Malaysia."

He fell silent, navigating through the traffic. "That was so long ago. I haven't— you haven't forgiven me for that still, have you?"

"Have I forgiven my father? Has my father forgiven me?"

"And yet you still want to will him half of our property? I don't get it."

"You wouldn't get it, Christopher," she said, staring out the window. "It's not about forgiveness. It's about obligation. I wouldn't be who I am without him."

"But that's just it. You *are* who you are without him."

"It's cultural. You wouldn't understand."

"How many times in the last twenty-odd years have I heard that?"

"You don't even know how long we've been married!"

"Nkiru. Be reasonable."

"You should thank your British stars I was reasonable enough to abandon my parents for you!"

"To God be the glory!" he muttered under his breath.

* * *

"Surprise me!" Nkiru was not impressed.

That night he slept on the couch in his study.

"Don't screw with Mom," Victor said at breakfast the next morning. "She'll—"

"Mind your tongue, young man," his parents said, almost in unison. Nkiru added, "Shut up this your dirty mouth."

The final will named Nkiru's sister and parents as limited beneficiaries. "Let them know at least if I die that I haven't forgotten them," she said. She had it written in that she should be buried in the family plot in her father's village.

"Are you sure?" Christopher asked. When she nodded, he looked at the line for his burial site and had Loestine write

Now, as Nkiru slowly spins around in his chair, with Jen away in the kitchen, she nurses a sudden urge to examine a place she hardly enters. Christopher's study is crisp and clean, no wrinkles in his Persian rug, papers in appropriate stacks, in file cabinets, but none of the organization in here has any particular order. In those cabinets, Victor's report cards mix with company documents, their tax statements with back issues of the *Economist*. He always said "I know how I put things. I can find what I need." And he could.

Nkiru begins with the desk, pulling each drawer out and flicking through its contents haltingly, looking over her shoulder as if expecting him to storm in. There are bills and receipts, Victor's high-school graduation program, a lost pair of Magdalene College cuff links and three half pairs of gloves.

Jen walks in with two cups of tea. "Thought you might like some," she says. For the first time Nkiru notices what a pretty woman Jen is. Graying hair yes, wrinkles yes, but there's something in the oval shape of her eyes, in the smallness of her mouth with its dimpled lips. Jen sits on the floor cross-legged with the couch as a backrest. Nkiru swivels to face Jen and pulls her knees to her chest.

"How do you sit like that?" she asks.

"Yoga. Bill and I do yoga."

"Bill? Yoga?"

"Well, he is a professor of philosophy," she laughs. Nkiru smiles.

"I always wanted Christopher to exercise. I had an exercise room put in in the basement when he was away, once."

"Really?"

"Yes. But only Victor and I use it. He never had the time, or so he said."

Jen nods. "Oh, I've heard that many times before."

"Maybe I'll try it. Yoga."

"Oh, you should. God, it helps for the ER. Calms you down." Nkiru rocks back and forth, listening to the dry rustle of her own braids. "Here, let me show you," Jen says, scanning the room for an empty spot. She stands up. "Can I?" she asks, already pushing with her backside against the couch. Nkiru gets up to help, and slowly the couch scrapes along the floor. "What's that?" Jen asks, pointing to a panel on the wall.

Nkiru bends down, examining the cracked paint and the darker metal showing through at the hinges. She pulls forcefully on the latch and falls back against Jen's legs, the panel flapping against the wall with a wobbly metallic *klang*, manila envelopes falling to the floor, some of them showing other envelopes protruding from their mouths. They are too stunned to move.

"Ah ah! What's this?" Nkiru asks. She reaches for the thickest of the fallen envelopes and sits down on the couch. Jen picks up the rest. "Jen. I'm scared," Nkiru whispers. "I'm so scared." She starts to cry, Jen next to her now, holding her. "What if? What if? He was cheating on me? Having an affair?" She sniffles loudly and tries to speak over the snot caught in her throat.

"Don't be ridiculous, Nkiru—he wouldn't! And would he hide the evidence in the house?"

"But he's been acting so strange in here, so secretive sometimes. On the phone…" She starts to sob. "No, Christopher. Not again."

"Give it to me," Jen says, working the envelope loose from Nkiru's hand. "Come on. Let's see…" She opens it, and then one of the smaller envelopes inside.

From this she pulls out two stapled sheets folded in perfect thirds. The top is a photocopy of Christopher's loopy script, the bottom a meticulously printed response in blue ink on unlined paper. Jen opens the other white envelopes, all of them, to reveal the same, though the letters get thicker and their folds less perfect. The most recent one has three British Airways tickets. "Nkiru! Look—look!" Jen says, pulling her head up and forcing the tickets under her nose. Nkiru's head jolts back.

"When is Victor's spring holiday?" Christopher asked her a week before.

They stood in the kitchen, he chopping vegetables and she washing cubes of stew-cut beef. "Why?" she asked. The meat clunked into the pot. "Well," Christopher ventured, "I was thinking. I have a trip to Malaysia coming up." Nkiru's eyes widened. She began to wash her hands, scrubbing them the way she would for surgery. "And I wanted—I wanted to take Victor to K-L with me."

"Oh. That's nice," she said, and went quiet.

"He's never been before."

"I've never been to K-L before," she said.

"Hmm?" he asked, his cell phone by his ear. "Victor? It's Dad... no, no. Everything's just fine. How's the reading going? Stressful? Chin up. Only a week more of exams and then—oh, you're going skiing.

Where? Vermont? They've got good skiing there? Didn't think so. Listen, Victor, before you dash off—your mum and I wanted to know the dates of your spring holiday. Twenty-second through April first. That's not long. Didn't you used to get more time? Ah, secondary school. Not university. I see. Okay—okay. Love you. 'Bye."

"Pardon?" he asked. "You were saying?" He looked up at his wife.

"Never mind," she mumbled.

"Oh—well, why don't you come? I didn't ask—well—for obvious reasons. And I didn't know if you could get time off."

"I can have time off," she said, almost too quickly. She turned to the stove to fiddle with the dials.

"Brilliant." The vegetables hissed when they hit the oil.

The next day she told him she had rearranged her schedule. "You're sure about this?" he asked. "You really want to come with us?"

Nkiru nodded.

"Okay then. I'll buy the tickets," Christopher said. And that was the last he was able to say about it.

The tickets are dated March twenty-first. Washington-Dulles, London-Heathrow, and then Lagos, Nigeria. The letters are addressed to her father, the first one from the same day they signed the will. It's brief, businesslike—*Long time... given your daughter's, my wife's wishes to be buried in the family plot in Nigeria... I thought I would write to establish contact on this particular issue...*

"Why didn't you tell me?" Nkiru wails.

The response from her father, in the printing she had copied years ago, at their dining table—*Dear Mr. Watsman... shock of a life... my daughter is she all right? Is she near death? Please let me know the news...*

"Why wouldn't he tell me?"

With each letter, the formality fades, the familiarity grows. *I should have come to you for permission, but... I shouldn't have pushed her out, but... Would she speak to me now? Do you think... My son is at Harvard...*

My grandson. He is a bright young man then. He takes after his mother and his father also I am sure.

It's night by the time Nkiru reaches the last one, swallowing hard and smacking her lips. "You don't mean it," she repeats, reading her father's words—*I am an old man and I have made many mistakes, but before I die, I want only to see my daughter again. Please how can we arrange...*

The tickets are still in her hand. What would I have done if he'd told me, she wonders, Christopher. Aiwo!

Jen rubs Nkiru's back. "It's okay, baby. It's okay."

For now, Nkiru thinks. It's okay for now. But by tomorrow Victor will know that his father is dead.

JOHN BRANDON'S novel, *Arkansas*, is out from McSweeney's now, or very soon. For more on him, please see the back of this book.

AMANDA DAVIS was raised in Durham, North Carolina, and lived in New York City and Oakland. She is the author of *Circling the Drain*, a collection of short stories, and *Wonder When You'll Miss Me*, a novel. She died in 2003.

MICHAEL GILLS's first book, *Why I Lie: Stories*, was chosen by the *Southern Review* as a top literary debut of 2002. He was a Randall Jarrell Fellow in the MFA program at the University of North Carolina at Greensboro, and earned a PhD in Creative Writing at the University of Utah. Work from his new book of stories, *The Death of Bonnie and Clyde*, has recently appeared in the *Oxford American*, *Verb*, the *Chattahoochee Review*, and other fine places. He teaches writing in the honors department at the University of Utah.

WAYNE HARRISON lives in Eugene, Oregon, with his beautiful wife and their brand-new daughter. His stories have appeared in *Ploughshares*, *New Letters*, and *Other Voices*, and he's hard at work on a novel about mechanics in the northwest who make ends meet by selling cannabis in large quantities.

UZODINMA IWEALA is the author of the

novel *Beasts of No Nation*. His short stories have been published in the *Paris Review* and *Granta*, and he now attends Columbia University College of Physicians and Surgeons.

Ismet Prcic is Bosnian-American. He's currently attending UC Irvine and writing a book called *Shards*, excerpts of which have appeared in *Cheese + Liquor* and the *Prague Literary Review*.

OUR FUTURE ISSUES

ISSUE 27

Plunging straight into the grayish, faintly understood area of the art world that involves oddly drawn objects coupled with uncertainly spelled text, McSweeney's 27 brings together a previously uncategorized cadre of pithy draftsmen, genius doodlers, and fine-artistic cartoonists, and buffets them with essays examining just what it is that these people are doing and why the world should know about it. With a sketchbook by Art Spiegelman, and work by David Shrigley, Tucker Nichols, and many other excellent artists.

ISSUE 28

In eight illustrated books, elegantly held together in a single beribboned case, McSweeney's 28 explores the state of the fable—those astute and irreducible allegories one doesn't see so much anymore in our strange new age, when everyone is wild for the latest parable or apologue but can't find time for anything else. Featuring fable-length work by Daniel Alarcón, Sheila Heti, and Nathan Englander, and different illustrators for each piece, McSweeney's 28 promises to offer many nights' worth of fine reading.

Subscribe now at store.mcsweeneys.net, or by calling 415-642-5684. Still only $55 for a year.